TAKE A CHANCE ON ME

ON ME

M.J. Schiller

Published By Kissmet Publishing

CHAPTER ONE

Five-Foot-Two-Eyes-Of-Blue. That's what he'd been calling her for weeks. Cash Delmonaco slid into the end seat at a blackjack table, where he could keep an eye on the suspect, although that wasn't where his attention was focused at the moment. He watched her hands—beautiful, graceful— as the cards arced like a rainbow between them. They slapped onto the table, one at a time, intermixing like couples at a speed dating event, the noise satisfyingly sharp. Like his nerves. And not because he was investigating a "probable" prostitution ring with "possible" mob tie-ins that was "likely" laundering money. Yeah, Victory, New York might not be Vegas, but vice wasn't picky about locations. Vice went where the action was. Where the money was. But he'd be damned if that happened on his watch. He wanted, *needed* to keep this town clean. In memory of his parents.

But all that aside, his pulse wasn't racing because he was some action junkie cop. His adrenaline was fueled by what would affect any red-blooded male. Her. He lifted his head, his gaze traveling over delicate wrists, up her arms, and across the swell of her breasts. Her chest was draped in black

3

silk, the skin hidden from view, although the way she filled the material tantalized him. She had a perfect column of a neck. He paused, imagining his lips brushing along the hollow there. After a few seconds, his view continued to climb. An appealing full mouth, flawlessly shaped. China-doll skin, and—BAM!—those eyes. Bluer than the waters of the Greek isles, which he'd only seen in pictures.

She must have felt him looking at her because she raised her head and their gazes connected. His smile was automatic, involuntary. She drew in a breath and her hands faltered, a card squirting out of the pack, soaring halfway across the table. She snatched it off the green felt, sliding it back into the fold while peeking over her shoulder. The move didn't escape her pit boss's attention and the large Asian man raised his eyebrows, arms crossed, frowning at her.

"Sorry," she said demurely without looking up. "It won't happen again."

He growled but moved on to the next table.

She rolled a shoulder as if pushing back the chill of his disapproval and gave herself a slight shake, suddenly nothing but business. "All bets down?" She skimmed her painted fingernails over the table, checking that everyone had their chips in place, then dealt.

Her table was always full. And it was no wonder. The ultimate combination of girl-next-door and sex kitten. Who wouldn't want to take cards from her? Even when the cards were as weak as a nine and a three, when the dealer showed a two, which was the case at the moment. He knew a player was always supposed to assume the dealer's under card was a ten, as it had the highest chances to be a ten, with all the face cards equaling that value. That would mean, if he stayed with his twelve, he would at least bump, and not lose any money. And if he took a card, he would likely end up with a ten, giving him twenty-two, and he would bust, losing the hand. But there were also a whole lot of combinations she could have that would beat his twelve....

He felt Ian behind him rather than saw him. The

result of partnering for so long.

"You've got to hit on that," he whispered.

"Shut up."

She'd finished with the other players, who all seemed to have good cards. He was up.

Throwing a look over her shoulder again, she leaned in, close enough he could catch her scent. Apple pie and leather. The paradox fit.

"Your friend's right," she murmured.

He raised his head. Her eyes showed laughter.

If he tipped his chin and moved an inch, those lips would be his. Not the best move, though. Might seem a bit forward, seeing as they'd never met.

Ian bent to speak into his ear, his gaze on the dealer. "I've heard it said you're more likely to lose your heart at La Bonne Chance than your money. After tonight, I'd have to say they're right. A lot of these dealers are lookers."

But there's only one I'm looking at.

But why's he *looking at her?*

His partner, though married now, had been a ladies' man in his day, and if he'd do anything, Cash would keep him away from this dealer. He swiveled in his chair and glared at his friend.

Ian held up his hands. "Okay. Okay." He walked away.

With a sigh, Cash gestured for another card, and she flipped it over. A nine. Twenty-one. Things were looking up. She smiled and nodded. Dimples, too. He was a goner.

She turned over a five and dealt herself an eight. *Bust.* Everyone cheered, and she paid up. He put down a two-chip tip for her and checked on the suspect. The huge African-American guy looked like he was stuffed into his impeccable black suit. His electric blue tie, perfectly knotted, must be special ordered to fit his tree trunk neck. *Why is everyone a behemoth in here?* Cash had passed him earlier and noted a flat nose that he always seemed to be looking down, and small, close-set eyes. A gold nametag read Lewis DePesto,

Floor Supervisor, Detroit, Michigan.

The big man pulled out a chair at the bar for a slender woman whose jet-black hair was drawn up in a sleek bun. Sparkling jewelry dripped from her ears and neck. Her almond eyes were outlined expertly, with that whole smoky thing going on, which he found so appealing. The Lewis guy had one hand on her chair and the other on the back of the adjacent seat, whose occupant turned toward the woman. The guy next to her possessed all the parts to be attractive, he guessed—dark thick hair, white smile, yada yada—but the pieces weren't meshing as they should. He was off. Geeky looking instead of slick. He dressed expensively, but not well, unable to pull the clothes together either. She was *way* out of his league.

"Sir? Do you want to hit?"

"What?" He swiveled back and glanced at his cards. A four and a jack. Fourteen. "Yeah, hit me."

She hesitated long enough for him to know he'd made the wrong play. He looked at her hand. She showed a six. Odds said she would bust.

"I'm sorry. I didn't quite hear you above that lady celebrating her jackpot at the slots." A fifty-some-year-old with bottled red hair screamed and jumped up and down like a lunatic. "I need you to give a clear gesture for the cameras."

He waved another card off, flashing her a smile of gratitude for the second chance, then turned his attention back to the bar. The couple was gone. His heart rate picked up. He searched the floor and spotted her red dress as they slipped into an elevator.

Ian flew in from out of nowhere and stuck his hand between the closing doors to join them. *Covering my ass again. I'll have to buy him a brew for that one.*

"Sir, are you in?"

He moved a couple of chips into the circle on the table across from his chair, and she dealt. He slid his gaze to the bar again. Something had caught his attention earlier. A tall blonde with an up-do similar to the other woman's. She

6

wore an electric blue curve-hugging dress in the same style as the first woman's.

"Do you want a card?"

Her voice had an edge.

"Hmm… Yeah, yeah. I'll take a card." This time he remembered to gesture, tapping the table. He was vaguely aware of the groan from the other players a second or two later. Five-Foot-Two—*I need to quit calling her that. Even if it is only in my head*—raked in his chips. No big deal. His captain had supplied him with gambling money. He'd put in his own if necessary. He glanced at her nametag.

Harper from St. Louis, Missouri. *Well, Harper from St. Louis, I'd love to find out more about you than just your name and state of origin.*

She didn't seem to be aware of his ogling, as she was busy laying out the cards. That red hair of hers, shimmering in the casino's lights, was enough to force the lust to rush through his veins. Remembering he was supposed to be working, he tore his focus from her and studied the girl in blue again.

The jewelry matches, too.

He took in the rest of the room.

And my guy Lewis is leading some schmuck there. This one's practically bald and twice her age. Could they be any less subtle?

Minutes later, they rose and headed for the elevators like the other pair. Either these guys were getting incredibly lucky—which he doubted—or money was exchanging hands.

He realized everyone at the table was staring at him. His play. He gestured, and her card flipped before she again took his money.

Or maybe that bartender's serving one mean love potion. I could use some of that for Five-Foot-Two.

Harper! The girl has a name.

The only people at the bar now were a group of guys doing shots. He scanned the area for his suspect and caught him near the elevators, standing with his feet wide, shoulders back, one hand circling the wrist of his other, both resting on his stomach. His gaze skipped about the room, and Cash had to look away when it neared him.

"Insurance?"

A glance back at the table told him Harper had an ace. Thinking insurance was a chump's bet, he declined, as did everyone else at the table. The other card turned out to be the jack of spades. A true blackjack.

Swell. As she dealt the next hand, a woman approached Lewis. She wore her blonde hair down, straight, and a red halter style dress caressed her body. No jewelry. They talked, looked toward the bar, and she nodded and moved in that direction.

Cash checked his cards. He had eighteen. Good hand this time. Maybe he'd win some back.

Eying the bar again, he noticed the "lady in red's" legs were crossed, the top one bouncing up and down like a Superball. A girly martini sat in front of her as she leaned on the bar with her elbows, staring off into space. She sat on the opposite side of the square bar from the pack of guys, but they zeroed in on her. One straightened his shirt and took a few steps in her direction, but two of his friends grabbed his arms and dragged him back and they all had a good laugh about it.

Murmurs and the scuffling of chairs moving alerted him. She had a friggin' pair of kings. No way.

"Sorry, guys. Enjoy the rest of your time at La Bonne Chance. And come back and see us again."

As his friends discussed their next move, one of the players leaving separated from the herd. Leaning forward, he rested an arm on the table. "What time do you get off, Harper?"

Her eyes widened. "Umm...I'm not sure."

He frowned. "Not sure what time you get off?"

Cash followed the conversation while trying to appear as though he wasn't. The guy looked like the putz at the bar earlier, only his pieces were coming together just fine. Cash gritted his teeth.

"Well…I'm scheduled off at ten, but sometimes they make me stay later. I get a break at nine, though."

"Then why don't you join me for a drink during your break?"

"Uhh…we're not allowed to drink on the clock. And the break's too short anyway."

"Then how about I wait for you until ten over at that bar?" He tilted his head in its direction and swept an arm toward it, too.

What is this jackass doing? She's not interested in him.

Harper hesitated, biting her bottom lip.

Is she?

"We're not supposed to…fraternize with the clientele, sir."

"You can call me Jim. And we're not fraternizing." He glanced at the pit boss, closing the gap between Harper and him even more. "I'm just going to buy a pretty lady a drink, on her own time. What can they say to that?"

Cash stopped breathing, leaning forward a fraction to catch her answer.

The pit boss circled around behind her like a shark in a tank, before stopping to loom over her. She scrambled to deal a hand to Cash and an old drunk at the other end of the table who looked like he was napping.

"I can't," she whispered hoarsely.

Her Don Juan, safe behind the comfort of the table, looked at the boss boldly. Like he could take the three hundred-fifty pounder. He'd be killed. "I'll be right over there, angel." With one last glare at the big man, he threw her a wink and headed off. A false show of bravado, or stupidity? It was hard to say.

Harper exhaled as he walked away and suddenly seemed a whole lot smaller. And vulnerable.

Cash's gaze drifted to the boss, then back to her.

"So, Harper from St. Louis, how long have you

worked here?"

"A couple of months." She smiled. "Does it show?"

"No, no. You're doing a great job. A real pro."

She won again.

Crap.

He sucked in a breath through his teeth. "Maybe too good."

Movement in his peripheral vision alerted him. The blonde was up and moving.

"You'd lose less if you weren't so busy looking at her."

He swiveled back to Harper. "Oh, no. Her? No. I just—"

"Save your breath." She shifted and looked beyond him. "She *is* gorgeous." She was flushed and her jaw was tight. Did having Jim wait for her upset her?

She turned to stare at the older guy on the stool for a beat. A soft snore issued from his mouth. She shook her head with a small smile and dealt to Cash, leaving the old man's spot empty.

I should get up and move to a busier table where I have more time to scope out the scene without getting caught.

He looked at her again. She pushed a strand of hair behind her ear. Damn. Even her ears were cute. His heart went into rocket mode. He wasn't going anywhere.

She reached the white card one of the players stuck in the deck that told her it was time to shuffle. It was that Jim prick who put it there. *What? Was he taking it as foreplay when she asked him to cut the deck? She'd probably asked a zillion guys to cut it before, including the snorer.* As she removed the cards from the shoe in order to shuffle, he checked to see if ol' Jimbo was really at the bar.

Yup. Loser.

Harper cleared her throat. "So you know my name. What's yours?"

She looked at the cards.

"Cash."

10

"Cash," she sputtered, stopping mid-shuffle. "If you were giving me a fake name, at least you could come up with something more original than that." She shook her head. "Cash. The Card Player."

He laughed. "No. I swear. My mama was a huge Johnny Cash fan. Sang me 'Folsom Prison Blues' as a lullaby."

"Nothing like shooting a man to watch him die to put a baby to sleep."

He laughed. He liked her quick wit and the twinkle of fun that never seemed to leave her eye.

"Your mama had good taste though. That's an awesome song."

"It is. One of my favorites. Behind 'Sweet Child of Mine.'"

She looked him straight in the eye. "I love that song." She had a habit of engaging with him, then glancing away. Perhaps to avoid *fraternizing*. "And you know, I shouldn't tease about the name. My mom was a huge reader. Guess what my last name is."

Harper…what was the name of that chick who wrote To Kill a Mockingbird*?*

"Lee."

"Nope. Good guess, though. Mine's worse. Harper Collins."

It took him a second. "Like the publisher?"

She nodded.

"Man!"

She laughed. "I told you."

Cash took a drink of his Captain and Coke, which he'd forgotten he even had. She was doing a thorough job of shuffling. Something his aunt would have irritably called, in her deep smoker's voice, "Shuffling the face off the cards." Maybe his sweet little dealer didn't want the conversation to end either. He played with his chips as he studied her, picking them up, then letting them drop, enjoying the clinking sound. He straightened the increasingly short pile before lifting a few again.

"So what brought you all the way from St. Louis to the blustery North?"

She tipped her head to the side and laid out his cards. "A mistake. Would you like a card, Cash?"

Her demeanor had changed again. Shoulders slumped, spark gone out of her eyes. *A mistake?* He chewed on that for a while. *What kind of mistake?* The shadow of her boss darkened the table, and he hurried to signal for a card and busted. She ended up with a soft seventeen. If he'd stayed, she would have most likely busted, or at least he would have bumped and kept his money.

"Sorry."

He grinned. "Yeah. Sure you are."

The smile was back, though weaker. The man at the other end of the table made a particularly loud snore and woke himself with a shake.

"What? Hmm?" He blinked.

She put a hand on his arm. "Hey, Joe. Maybe it's time to go home to Martha."

He rubbed a hand over his face. "Yeah. You're probably right. Thanks, Harper." He collected himself, taking several seconds to come to a full standing position, like his spine was made out of Jell-O.

"You're catching a cab?" Her voice was soft whenever she spoke to him.

"Oh, yeah. You know me. Smart about DUIs. Dumb about cards."

"Oh, no. You know your cards, all right." She nodded sharply. "Lady Luck just wasn't with you tonight."

He looked at Cash, the corners of his lips lifting. "Well, Lady Luck is a—and excuse me for saying this young lady—bitch!" He winked.

Cash chuckled. "She definitely can be." He could tell the kindly older man was somewhat of a character.

"Well," Joe shuffled forward, "I hope you have better luck tonight." He tipped his head toward Harper and put a hand on Cash's arm, turning sideways and leaning in. "Take care of this pretty little lady."

Cash jerked. Was he that obvious? "I'll do what I can," he whispered back.

Joe laughed until he wheezed. "Oh, I'm sure you will."

"Hey. What's with all the whispering?" Harper interjected.

The old man shuffled off, throwing a "Never you mind," over his shoulder and still chuckling. "That's between me and Cash."

He knows my name? Old codger's not as out of it as he seems to be.

Harper frowned. "What did he say?" She was more animated now.

Cash put up a hand. "You heard Joe. It's between him and me."

She watched the old man retreat over his shoulder. "Oh," she huffed. "Whatever. Ante up."

He put his bet in and threw a glance at the bar, almost out of reflex now. Jim was still there, but the blonde joined him. She had a martini on the bar in front of her, as well as an empty glass. She looked a lot…peppier. Jim bent to say something in her ear and she laughed, putting a hand on his shoulder. He drew back, but only a little. He had an elbow on the bar and moved a hand to her knee, stroking her, but casting a look in Harper's direction at the same time. He seemed torn.

Cash returned his concentration to his hand and, having nineteen, upped his bet. She drew a twenty and he reached for his chips for the next round, only to find he was out of them. He dug into his pocket for his wallet. Time for him to play on his own dime. He laid a fifty-dollar bill on the felt, and she converted it to chips, her hands doing the choreographed dance all dealers did. Stacking his chips, measuring them against the next pile, and pouring them out on the table. Finally, she put his bill in the slot near her and

13

pushed it down with the paddle.

A half hour and thirty dollars later, she seemed to sense the new dealer behind her like he had Ian. Nine o'clock. Time for her break. She tipped her head, turning her palms up for the cameras. Cash checked out the couple at the bar. When he turned back, Harper shook her head. "Maybe you should just ask her out."

Cash leaned forward, trying to give her his most charming smile. "Maybe it's not her I want to ask out."

She blinked and seemed about to say something when the pit boss hovered. She looked down. "It was nice meeting you, Cash."

He took his chips and scrambled to his feet. "Time for your break?"

She checked over his shoulder. "I'm off now. I lied to that Jim guy to get him out of my hair. I'm going to try to duck out without him seeing me." She gave him a smile. "Hope your luck turns. Have a good night." The pit boss grabbed her elbow as she turned to leave. "You're not here to flirt."

She snatched her arm back, rubbing it. "I understand that." Her tone was defensive, but she dropped her chin and scurried off. Cash hoped he didn't get her in trouble.

"Are you in, sir?" The new dealer smiled at him.

He watched Harper weave through the crowd to an unmarked door. "No. I'm sitting this one out."

CHAPTER TWO

Harper balanced, one hand against the wall, and slipped out of her shoes. Her feet were killing her. She continued padding down the deserted hall to the break room to clock out, shoes in her hand. The cool tile was refreshing, as was the opportunity to distribute her weight more evenly, rather than all on the balls of her toes. It was only a couple minutes after nine, but to her it felt like two o'clock in the morning. Who knew that, at the ripe old age of twenty-four, one could be so bone tired.

As she reflected on her evening, her feet slowed. Her answer to "Cash's" question kept reverberating in her mind.

So what brought you all the way from St. Louis to the blustery North?

A mistake.

Jared was a mistake, all right. A painful, bank-draining mistake. One she was still paying for.

And what about that "Cash?" He was definitely yummy. A gorgeous face, strong jaw covered in a shadow that was something more than stubble, but less than beard. He rubbed his chin in this sexy way when he thought. Goose pimples practically broke out over her arms remembering it. Or he'd put his hand over his mouth and mustache, raising his eyebrows as he stared at his cards. A mouth with nice, full lips.

Mmm...

He wore his sideburns long, as well as the hair on top, which either fell rakishly over his forehead, or was swept to the side by a big, strong hand. It lay perfectly. He must have a good stylist. Lucky girl. She sighed. She'd love to run her hand through those dark layers. Love to feel those lips work their magic. Love to run her hands up his thigh and—

Stop. Just stop. He's a mistake. He's some other woman's mistake.

But another voice rose in her.*But it can't hurt to fantasize about him.*He'd sat with one booted foot on the floor, the other on the rung of his stool, swung out a little, casual. Relaxed. It was hard to judge his height at first, but when she left, she threw a look back. He was pocketing his chips. Looked to be about a foot taller than her, between six-one and six-three. He wore a black button-down and his jeans were snug and faded in the right places.

Oh, my God. What an ass. Tight.

She bit her lip, giggling. The more she thought about it, the more she realized, above everything else, it was his eyes. Startlingly blue, both set off and framed by his other dark features, drawing her in. They had a devilish twinkle at times. And sometimes looked at her so intensely her knees felt weak and she had to lean against the table a little to stay upright.

But he kept looking over to the bar. Checking out the women there. Like a powerful lion sifting through the herd for the one who would be his tonight.

A definite mistake. And a definite shame.

Her heart skipped when the door crashed open behind her, and she spun, afraid Jim might have found her out.

She pressed a hand against her chest. "Kitty! You scared the shit out of me!"

Her best friend and roommate barreled toward her. The tall, willowy blonde waited tables in one of the casino's restaurant.

"Sorry. You off? Let's get out of here." Kitty's words

ran together. When she reached Harper, she grabbed her arm, swinging her around. She dragged Harper along with her, gripping her elbow.

In the obscenely bright lights of the hallway, her friend's face looked drawn and pale. "What's wrong?"

Kitty glanced over her shoulder. "Nothing. I just want to go." Her eyelashes fluttered.

They always did that when she was upset about something. Something was up. But her lethargic mind couldn't quite catch up with what was happening. "But...I thought you worked until twelve."

They'd reached the end of the hallway. "I'm taking off early. Where's your car?"

"In the front. But, didn't you bring your own car?"

"Yeah. Yeah. Let's go out this way." She pushed the bar on the door at the end of the hall.

"Isn't it kind of creepy this way?"

They stepped out onto a concrete platform. Instead of the fresh air that might be expected, they were met with a stagnant wall. They were deep in the bowels of La Bonne Chance's parking garage, in a section that wasn't used much. All of the taxi and limo stands were in the area closer to the front of the casino.

Harper leaned on the metal railing at the edges of the four-by-four-foot slab of concrete they stood on to wedge on her heels. Having been briefly released from the confines of her shoes, her feet had swelled, making it difficult to put the heels back on. "I'm not sure if two women by themselves should be—"

Kitty tugged on her arm, trying to lead her down the short staircase to the garage floor. "Come on, Harp. It's fine."

She hopped around on one foot. "Wait, Kitty! I've got to get my shoes on."

"Oh." Kitty stared at her as if just realizing she was shoeless.

"Geez. What's up with you?"

Kitty opened her mouth, but closed it again, not

offering any explanation. "Got 'em on?" She turned her head to scope out the area while waiting.

"Yes." Harper started to follow her friend down the steps, but turned back. "Wait a sec. I forgot to clock out."

Kitty made an impatient sound.

"It'll only take a minute. Just wait for me here. Don't go anywhere by yourself. Okay?" She hesitated, unsure her friend would listen to her in the hurry she was in.

"Yes. Okay. Okay. Go clock out."

Harper would snap back at Kitty were she not so concerned about her. She whirled to head inside. Luckily, the door didn't close all the way. "Two seconds." She ran into the break room, which was empty, and punched out. As predicted, when she hit the landing again, Kitty was gone. Harper turned toward the stairs and heard voices. Fifty yards away, her roomie stood speaking to four men. The murky light made it impossible to see their faces. One man stood a bit ahead of the others. His pristine suit and tie, along with his perfectly gelled red-blond hair, made him look out of place in the dirty garage. Without warning, he raised a gun and shot Kitty point-blank in the chest. The explosion of noise bounced off the walls and hit Harper like shrapnel. Kitty staggered backward, and he shot again. And again. And again. With each shot, she jerked like she was on the end of a mad puppeteer's strings. The final shot launched her body into the concrete wall behind her. She slid down, leaving behind a wide streak of blood.

A choking noise escaped Harper's mouth. Somewhere between a scream and a cough. Four heads turned at the same time. The man who shot Kitty still held the gun. He made eye contact with Harper.

"She saw!" He raised his gun and fired. A bullet whizzed past her.

For an instant Harper didn't react, but the men running toward her finally produced a reflexive response. She turned and yanked on the handle of the door, but this time it had shut and locked behind her. A bullet pinged off the iron bar at her side. Pulse racing, she bent and swung under the back section of the rusty railing, then dropped a decent distance to the ground, breaking the heel of one of her shoes. Another bullet hit the top of the railing she hung from an instant earlier. She ripped her shoes off and ran blindly into the depths of the garage. Feet pounded behind her, shots were fired, men shouted. Her heart hammered. The concrete under her feet was rough, cutting through her hose and her skin. A sob ripped from her. In her mind, she kept seeing Kitty fall.

They shot her! They shot her! Oh, my God, they shot her!

The garage sloped downward the farther in she got. *Ping.* A bullet bored through a dumpster ahead of her. She ducked into the shadows near the building. Were there any amount of light she would have been hit. She knew that. She could hear her pursuers closing the gap, but they were no longer shooting.

Where was she going to go? It was only a matter of time before they caught up. Tires squealed, and she turned her head to look back. Three silhouettes ran in her direction. She was caught in a car's headlights. They would see her now. A white-hot fear pulsed in her chest. The car's engine roared.

She swiveled her head forward and had to blink away spots the headlights created in her vision. When it cleared, she saw it. Ahead. A sliver of light from a door that wasn't closed all the way. Her lungs and throat burned, but she had to get to that door. Her foot landed on something cylindrical, and she pitched forward but was able to right herself and keep running. She could hear them breathing now. They were close. She called on every muscle she had to spur her to that door. But they were on her. As she reached it, someone caught hold of her hair, but only the ends. It slipped through his fingers and the effort he made to lunge at her threw him off balance. He fell into the others giving her the extra second she needed to slip through the door and close it behind her. Fists battered the door and she backed away, terrified.

Eventually her mind understood they could not get through the metal door. They were only human. She swayed on her feet and reached out for the wall, sliding to the floor and bawling with her head on her knees, hands laced behind her neck. Her flight forced her to struggle to bring air into her lungs, and the crying made it worse. Peering through her legs, she saw blood on the floor and scrambled away from it in a panic, but, inexplicably it followed.

Blood. Kitty's blood.

She stared at it in horror until logic fought its way to her brain. It wasn't Kitty's blood. Kitty was too far away. She twisted her foot to look at the sole. Blood saturated what little of the shredded nylon was left and black pieces of gravel stuck out, along with the glint of glass. A noise drew her attention to the door. She pushed her way up the wall to her feet while staring at the door in disbelief. It jerked and she recognized the sound of metal on metal. They had a key! But how could they have a key? Deep voices argued.

"Come on! Come on!"

"I'm trying. Back off!"

Harper turned and ran down the hall, but she didn't even know where she was. All of the outer hallways looked the same. She rounded a corner and a big purple A-3 was painted on the door. She knew this place. This was the hall off the security office. She'd lost her purse a couple of weeks ago and had come here to claim it. A door on the left side of the hall led into the office, which could also be reached from the casino floor.

She reached the door and tried the handle, but it was locked. She beat on it but didn't wait. She opened the door to the casino, stepped out, and turned to her left to access the door there. When she burst into the room the poor gray-haired security officer jumped out of his seat so quickly he knocked it over.

"Miss Collins! My God! What's wrong?"

She stumbled into the room, letting the door close behind her. Her mind was incapable of forming any words except, "Kitty! Kitty!"

"What? Miss Carmichael? Is she in danger?"

She shook her head, trying desperately to get enough air behind her voice to make it intelligible. She wanted to cry. She wanted to break down and cry. But she couldn't. She needed to tell him what happened. He crossed the room and helped her over to his chair, righting it so she could sit.

"Now, honey. Calm down. Catch your breath. Then you can tell me what's wrong." He parked his rear on the counter in front of her. A bank of TV screens attached to it showed the action on the floor. "Here. Have a drink."

He handed her a half-empty water bottle and she slugged it down gratefully but the fire in her throat increased. It wasn't water, it was vodka. She sputtered and some of it dribbled out. She wiped the back of her hand across her mouth.

He chuckled. "Sorry. I should have warned you about—"

"Kitty. They shot Kitty."

His eyes bugged out. "What? Whoa, wait. What are you talking about?"

"These four men. They shot her, and they chased after me. She needs an ambulance. It's bad." Her hands were shaking so hard she was sloshing vodka out of the bottle. She set it on the counter.

"They followed you into the casino?"

She had to think to come up with an answer. It was like her mind was wading through fudge. "I'm not sure. I think so."

He stood, switching off the TVs. "All right. Listen up. You stay right here, and I'll get some help. You'll be safe. No one will be able to get to you. I'll lock the door behind me."

She nodded.

"Okay." He hesitated. "Don't move from here. I'll be

21

right back." He left, closing the door behind him and locking it, as promised.

His departure made it suddenly too quiet in the office. A clock ticked on the wall, one of those plain-looking clocks that looked like it belonged in a schoolroom. It felt odd. Out of place. Like it should not go on ticking when Kitty was…Kitty was…hurt. She had to hope for the best. Maybe she'd survived the attack somehow. Why would anyone shoot Kitty? She was funny, and kind, and…a tad crazy sometimes, but wasn't everybody?

Harper sniffled and looked around for a box of tissues. Reaching for it, she accidentally turned the screens back on. It startled her at first, but she didn't bother to turn them off. She blew her nose and got up to throw the tissue away. She wandered back to the chair and lowered herself into it.

Her head throbbed. Where was he? How long was he going to take? She didn't like being alone, knowing they were out there, even if the door was locked. Her heartbeat had finally come back to normal, and now it felt like it wasn't beating at all. She felt dead, her limbs heavy. Slouching into the chair, she wondered if she'd be able to stand if she had to.

Her gaze drifted to the TVs. She jolted to an upright position. On the rightmost monitor a head of curly hair caught her attention. She rolled her chair closer and he turned toward the camera. It was the man who had shot Kitty, talking to the older security guard who'd helped her and a floor supervisor named Lewis. Their faces were serious.

They're working together.

The shooter seemed to be the one in charge, by their posturing. He spoke again, and the other two men nodded and turned to walk off the screen.

A combination of adrenaline and sheer panic shot through her system, and she sprung to her feet. She rushed to the door and tugged, although she knew it was locked. It took a key to turn the deadbolt on both sides of the door. Her head whirled. The other door worked the same way. She was trapped.

Okay. Calm down. Calm down.

She paced. "Think!" she screamed at herself then wondered if she was coming unglued and if it even mattered at this point.

She didn't want to die.

A key. Maybe there's a spare key in the desk.

Harper sprinted across the room and yanked on the biggest desk drawer so hard it fell completely out, the contents spilling on the floor.

Oh, no.

She got on her hands and knees and frantically searched through paper clips, pencils and pencil shavings, and rows of staples, thumbtacks, and various other items. She fought tears out of her eyes. Now is not the time to cry. She fanned her hand across the floor, scattered the items to get a better view.

A key. A key. There has to be a key.

But she could find none. She didn't have time to thoroughly search the other drawers, but she wrenched each one open for a cursory glance.

What am I going to do? They'll be here any minute.

She desperately panned around the room looking for something, anything, she could use to defend herself. Coming out from behind the desk, she took a few steps forward and the door creaked open. The gargantuan frame of Lewis the Floor Supervisor came through the opening. He closed the door behind him.

"Miss Collins." He was completely calm. "Stu Hafley told me you had quite a scare. Why don't you tell me what you think you saw."

Her voice caught in her throat.

He approached slowly now, studying her. "Are you okay, Harper? That is your first name, right?" His voice was silky smooth.

She nodded but took a step back. She needed to pull

herself together. Her wits were all she had right now.

They won't shoot me in here. Even as loud as the casino floor is, someone would hear a shot.

She stared at the man. She desperately wanted to search again for a weapon, but was afraid to look away. She needed to know his next move, and didn't want him to know hers. Lewis filled her with terror. Even before she knew he worked for, or with, the man who shot her best friend. His size was so intimidating. She was sure he had more strength in his pinkie finger than she did in her whole body. So she couldn't overpower him. She'd have to outwit him.

"Why don't you take a seat."

Sitting was the last thing she wanted to do, but he made it sound like an order, not a request. She backed into a chair and sat, her frame rigid. He approached, resting one butt cheek casually on the counter in front of the monitors.

"So, Harper, you—" He turned his head, dropping his gaze to the TVs. He froze for a moment, then sighed, spanning his forehead with a hand to rub his temples. "You know." He stood, towering over her. "Ahh… That's unfortunate." He dropped his professional attitude, laughing as he bent and took hold of both arms of the chair. He exhaled. "Listen, sugar. We can make this go real quick, or I can mess you up real bad. Your choice."

It didn't seem like much of one. She stared at him.

He straightened and swung off his suit coat, laying it carefully over the monitors. But he never moved more than a foot from her. He turned, rolling his sleeves. The overhead light caught the flash of the massive gold rings on his hands. Looking beyond him she realized he never locked the door. If she could get past him….

"You know what?" he asked conversationally, licking his lips. "I like it this way." He smiled. "Haven't had my workout today."

She bolted out of her seat and attempted to dodge around him, but his reach was longer than she expected. A thick arm grabbed her around the waist and hauled her in next to his body. The other arm snaked across her chest and his fingers closed around her shoulder. She thrashed, fighting him with everything she had.

"No! No! Let me go!"

His mouth was against her ear. "You're a fine looking woman, Miss Collins. A *fine* looking woman." He spun her around, holding her at arm's length. He ran his tongue over his teeth, his gaze sliding over her from head to foot. She felt naked. "Mmm. It's too bad we couldn't have gotten better acquainted." He chuckled. "You know what I mean?" He shoved her away from him then backhanded her so hard she flew across the desk, taking stacks of paper with her.

She lay still on the floor, moaning, papers floating down on top of her. She'd never been hit before in her life, and it hurt even more than she imagined. Through the gap between desk and floor, she saw his spit-polished shoes spin and walk out of sight. Her ears rung and her vision was going in and out. Hands clasped her waist and lifted her. She felt blindly under the desk and her fingers touched something cold, long, and hard. She pulled it in. A brass letter opener. It was so small compared to him, but it was all she had. She knew she would have only one chance to use it, so she needed to make it good. Her grip tightened on the letter opener.

He set her on her unsteady feet then spun her around. She raised her hand and swung it down as violently as she could, burying the letter opener in his chest up to her fingers. He sucked in a breath. Then, with a grimace, he plucked the opener out of his chest, flinging it across the room where it hit a wall.

"Ahh, now, that makes me mad."

Her stomach dropped. She knew making a dash for freedom was futile. Fight or flight, she was screwed. But she wasn't sitting there and making it easy for him either. She faked to the right and went left, but he wasn't fooled in the slightest. He scooped her up, hurling her against the wall, stomach first. He yanked her head back by her hair, then bashed it into the wall. She screamed in pain. Blood rolled down her forehead and nose, mixing with tears and sweat.

"You keep doing that." He pushed the side of her face against the wall, then laid his cheek on the wall opposite hers, taunting her. "No one out there's gonna hear you." He jerked her back, spun her like a dime on edge, then let her slump against the wall. She was exhausted, breathing hard, and unable to fight back any more. He put one hand on her shoulder, and gripped her chin. "So, should I snap your neck?" He brought his hands to her throat. "Or choke the life out of you? Huh?"

She thought about her parents and was sorry for all the grief she'd caused them. She thought about Kitty. And, sadly, she thought about Jared. The loser.

"You're not gonna answer me, baby girl?" He pulled her away then bashed her against the wall again. "Huh?"

"Just. Do it."

He laughed, and tightened his grip. "Yeah. I think I want to watch as the life slowly goes out of those pretty blue eyes of yours." He applied more pressure.

She sputtered, her head jerking around involuntarily. She thought she had nothing left to fight with, but as it turned out, when death came to introduce himself, emergency reserves clicked in. Not that it mattered.

"Huh. You're almost as blue as your eyes."

Her head was light. She imagined it was a balloon. Floating. Floating...

Her eyes rolled back in her head.

CHAPTER THREE

Cash stared into an empty wallet and decided maybe he wasn't as good at cards as he thought he was.

I was distracted.

But not by work. And it hadn't gotten any better since she'd left. He couldn't stop wondering about her answer to his question.

So what brought you all the way from St. Louis to the blustery North?

A mistake.

What kind of mistake could a beautiful girl like her make?

The dealer smiled at him. "Are you in?"

All in, but I'm not talking blackjack.

"Nah. I'm done." He stood, put his wallet back in his pocket, and was about to go look for Ian when he saw her. Harper stepped out on the floor and immediately turned to enter the security office. She looked distraught and disheveled. Was it that punk, Jim? He took off across the floor, but halfway there he stopped.

What am I going to be able to do? It's not like I can barge into the security office and ask, "What's up?"

But he knew something was wrong. He finished his walk across the casino and leaned against the wall, pretending to be texting.

An older security guard came out, locked the door,

then paused, rubbing a hand over his face and mumbling, "Holy shit."

Locking the door? Isn't she still in there?

"What's going on?" he said to himself in a sing-songy voice. There had to be another way in. If there was, it would be behind that door she came out of. He scanned the vicinity to see if anyone was looking his way and then slipped through the door. On his immediate right was a door with security marked over the top. He tried it, but it was locked. He walked the rest of the way down the hall, but saw no other doors. Worried he'd miss her coming out, he jogged back to reenter the casino.

After glancing around, he leaned against the wall again, stretching his feet out in front of him and sliding his hands in his pockets. He tapped one boot against the other and whistled tunelessly until he started to drive himself crazy and stopped. Coincidentally, the guy he was supposed to be watching was headed in his direction. He pushed off the wall and brought his phone out to fake text again.

Lewis the Bruiser, as he had nicknamed the hulking floor supervisor, strode up to the security door, unlocked it, and went inside, all without casting a glance in his direction. He looked…determined. Cash strolled across the floor, and acted like he was checking out a slot machine. He put one hand on the top of it, waited a few seconds, then casually peered in the direction of the security office. No one had come or gone. He tapped the top of the machine, his palms sweaty. Something was wrong. He could feel it. He slid out his phone and texted Ian.

SOMETHING UP WITH 5FOOT2. COULD USE HELP AT THE SECURITY OFFICE

He sent it, then remembered Ian wouldn't know where that was.

ACROSS FROM THE TABLE I WAS PLAYING

AT EARLIER

He got no response for a bit, then Ian texted:

ON MY WAY

But by that time, he was so on-edge he could taste it in his mouth. He had to know what was going on in that room. He formulated a plan, of sorts, then walked to the door and opened it, stumbling in.

"Oh, hi," he said with a sloppy grin, holding onto the doorframe as if it was the only thing keeping him upright.

The big man was breathing hard, and the room was pretty much a shambles, but there was no sign of Harper. They stared at each other.

"Did you need something?" Lewis asked pointedly.

"Yeah. I need to take a leak." He looked around, moving his body loosely. "But this isn't the boys' room is it?"

Is that blood on the wall?

"No. It's on the other side of the slot machines."

"Oh, yeah. Great." Cash started to close the door, but he thought he heard a cough that sounded female…if a cough could sound female. In any case, it didn't seem like it would come from big, barrel-chested Lewis. He swung the door wide again, pasting on the stupid grin. "Did you say something?"

A glimpse of red hair was visible over the top of the desk, positioned where Lewis' crotch would be.

"Uhh…me and my lady friend were trying to have an intimate moment…"

"Oh, geesh! Oh. I'll just…yeah." He backed out of the room feeling like he'd been sucker punched, closing the door behind him. He leaned on the doorknob. Harper and Lewis? No. It couldn't be. But he'd just seen it.

Wait.

What did I see?

She didn't move. At all. Didn't jump with the interruption or move a muscle.

Shit! Where's Ian?

He paced then realized he was drawing attention to himself and went over to sit in the slot machine's chair. He was about to break protocol and go in without backup when a big hullaballoo rose near the craps table. Two guys were shouting and squaring off. One landed a big roundhouse punch to the side of the other guy's head, knocking him against the table. A light above the door to the security office blinked. He guessed a second light must have been lit inside because Lewis came storming out.

He watched for a moment to make sure the big man was occupied. Now four or five guys were involved in the brawl, so it looked like the supervisor would be tied up a bit. He stood as Harper stumbled out of the door. She was hunched over coughing, one hand on her chest, the other out in front of her to feel her way. She moved jerkily in his direction.

"Harper?"

She lurched forward, wheezing, then straightened to plant her hands on his shoulders like she was doing a chest pass and shoved him. Caught off guard, he staggered backward, hit the chair, and fell over it. He flailed, managing to conk his head on the big ball at the end of the slot machine handle, which was surprisingly painful. He landed on his back, staring up as his mind tried to wrap itself around what happened. He noticed the ceiling actually had a pretty intricate pattern. Ian's face swam into his vision.

"What happened?"

He didn't think. His mind just spoke. "Five-Foot-Two."

Ian laughed. "No shit? That little puff of smoke knocked you on your ass?" He grasped his forearm and Cash's fingers closed around his in a similar fashion as Ian helped him to his feet. He held on and yanked Ian into him.

"If you ever tell anyone at the station about this—or

anyone else, for that matter—I'm gonna kick your ass," he growled.

"That would sound so much more convincing if you weren't waylaid by a girl half your size."

"Oh, shut up." Cash's gaze roamed about. "Did you see which way she went?"

"All I saw was you laying on the ground, flopping around like a fish out of water and—"

Cash punched him in the arm. "There was no flopping." He moved in the direction Harper headed.

"You sure had your mouth hanging open like a fish. Glug, glug, glug." He mimicked a wide-mouthed bass.

"You're an asshole. Look for blood," he threw over his shoulder. When she pushed him, he got a look at her face. She looked like a zombie from some B-movie, gray skin, crazy hair, and blood gushing from a gash above her eye. Cash picked up his pace but constantly searched the crowd for a sign of her. He figured she must have pressed something to that wound because there wasn't a drop of blood anywhere. After fifteen minutes of futile searching, he had to admit she could have gone anywhere. Stepping out onto the sidewalk of the busy thoroughfare in front of the casino, he looked one last time in both directions.

He exhaled, planting his hands on his hips and hanging his head for a second.

Ian gripped his shoulder. "We lost her."

"I know." He lifted his head. "Let's go back to the station and check in. You can start calling hospitals with a description of her on the way. That gash needs stitches."

***

Clearly Jerry Hayfield, manning the phones at the station, couldn't see Cash was in no mood to be messed with.

"Hey, Cash. I heard you let a girl clean your clock."

Cash's eyes widened and he turned to look at Ian, who shrugged, palms out. "Wasn't me, man."

"Ramirez and Nelson were there and saw the whole thing. Couldn't stop laughing." Jerry chuckled. "Wish I'da been there."

His booming voice caught the attention of half of the people in the squad room. He leaned back in his chair, hands interlaced behind his head, legs stretched out in front of him, crossed at the ankles. The buttons of his shirt strained and the spine of his chair creaked, already misshapen from repeated abuse. Cash briefly envisioned it snapping in half.

He strode toward Jerry, jaw clenched, until he knocked against wood. "Easy for you to say when you've got your jelly-donut-eating ass parked behind this desk." He was rewarded with laughter and a few "oohs."

Jerry's gaze darted around and returned to Cash. He frowned, bringing his hands from behind his head to grasp the edge of the desk and sit forward. "You think this is such an easy job, do ya?" His face was turning red and spittle formed at the corners of his mouth. "Bah. You wouldn't last an hour trying to handle the kooks I have to deal with every day."

Like a referee's whistle, the phone on his desk silenced both men. They stared at it briefly before Jerry said, "Well, go on, hotshot. Answer it."

Maintaining eye contact, Cash reached for the receiver with exaggerated slowness. "Fifth precinct, can I help you?" He annunciated his words carefully, raising his eyebrows at Jerry and smirking.

"They shot her. Right in front of me." The caller sobbed.

The argument with Jerry flew out of his mind and he was instantly focused on the call. He snatched a pencil and notepad off the desk and turned his back, tilting his head as if that would help him hear her better. "Who did?"

The question seemed to calm her a little. "I-I don't know. Some men. Four of them."

He scratched some notes. "And where did this take place?"

"At La Bonne Chance. In the back of the parking garage. Behind the building."

"Okay…" he wrote the information down, trying to formulate his next question.

"Why would anyone shoot Kitty?" She sounded truly bewildered, but the voice was familiar…

"Kitty?"

"Yes. Kitty Carmichael. She—"

The line went dead. Cash spun around. Jerry's finger was still pressing the base's switch hook, and he was holding his other hand out for the receiver.

"We don't do kitties up a tree. That's the fire department. Amateur." He rolled his eyes.

Heat flashed through Cash. "You idiot! That was a witness to a shooting!"

The blood drained from Jerry's face and his mouth opened and shut. "Umm. Umm…"

"Can you call that number back?"

"Yes." Jerry jumped to dial some numbers. "Is it ringing?"

Cash put the phone to his ear. At first he heard nothing, but it began to ring. He turned his back again. It rang. And rang. "Come on. Come on." After a bit he shut his eyes, sighing. He turned around, holding the handset out. "She's not answering. Can you trace that call?"

Jerry knit his eyebrows. "Maybe. But it'll take some time."

"Okay. Call me when you know where she is. Or was." He grabbed Ian's jacket as he walked past him. "Come on." He swiveled his head back. "Jerry. Get an ambulance and any unit close to La Bonne Chance into its back parking area."

Ian scrambled to keep up. "Where are *we* going?"

"Back to the casino." He'd finally figured out the voice. "That was Harper."

***

When they pulled up in their unmarked black
Mustang, the place was a circus. One uniformed cop was
trying to keep the crowd back. Bad news travels fast. Since
the ambulance was still there, Cash took it as a bad sign. He
blinked. The flashing lights of two police units and the
ambulance strobed around the walls, competing with each
other for attention.

He and Ian ducked under the crime scene tape.
Detective Mike Beason turned and spotted them. He spread
his arms wide as if to corral them and force them back under
the tape.

"Uhh-uh-uh. This is homicide, not vice."

"Might be related to our case," Cash bluffed.

Someone from the coroner's office and a crime scene
investigator turned at the disruption. He could see a black
body bag at their feet.

"So, she's dead?"

The M.E. nodded. "Four times over."

She waved him forward. As he got closer, he could
see it was Mitzi Hoffman. They'd worked together before.
He shook her hand.

"Cash. Good to see you." He nodded and she bent to
unzip the body bag.

Cash crouched, and mentally prepared himself. He
never got used to these scenes. He looked at the victim in her
bubble of black plastic. She was pretty. Young. Probably
close to his age....

Mitzi pointed with the corner of a small spiral
notebook she was holding to the neck. "This one was a
through and through. Would be fairly harmless except it
severed the spinal cord. Then at least three GSWs ripped
through the chest cavity, close-range, small caliber handgun.
No major artery seems to be hit, as evident by the lack of
blood splatter, but I suspect two of the bullets hit the heart.
Of course, I won't know for sure until I can open her up back
at the lab."

He stood, still looking down at the girl Harper called Kitty. She almost looked like she was sleeping. Mitzi moved the zipper back along its track and the gap closed over her face.

"Cash." Ian was at his elbow. "Look up."

A slight movement caught his eye so he was able to zero in on her right away. She was laying on her stomach on the floor above, peering over the edge. She immediately disappeared.

"Hey!" his voice echoed off the surrounding walls.

Cash ran, breaking through crime scene tape as he made it to the middle of the garage.

"You'll never catch her," Ian warned, but he ignored him.

He scrambled up the rows of cable between the levels meant to keep idiots like him from doing what he was doing. Using a column of concrete to his left to steady him, he climbed on the top cable, then had to balance for a moment before launching himself toward the next level up. He caught the cable one up from the bottom, but his lower body crashed into the concrete supporting the second floor. The impact forced most of the air out of his lungs and hurt like hell. He looked down, dangling now. He hadn't realized several floors sprawled below him as well. If he lost his grip, it wouldn't be pretty. He tried to use his feet, but they slid on the smooth wall at first. He curled his knees, bringing the shoes flat against the surface and used his body weight to hold him so he could let go with one hand and reach higher.

"You'll never catch her," Ian repeated, sounding bored.

Cash knew he was right, but he felt compelled to try anyway. He muscled his way up, walking along the wall like a web-slinging super hero, and finally was able to get his feet under the bottom cable and slide to the other side. Thanking his stars he didn't kill himself, *yet,* he jumped to his feet. She was nowhere in sight, but the only way she could go was up. He took off in pursuit. When he got to the top of his level, he looked left and right. Both sides had staircases. Which one would she take? Choosing left, he dashed across the expanse, flung the door open, and listened. Nothing.

"Damn!"

Reversing his steps, he hit the other staircase at a dead run. When his palm slammed into the metal bar to open the door, a shockwave radiated up his arm to his shoulder. He crossed to hang his head over the railing. She stopped before exiting through an outer door, seemingly to catch her breath. One hand was on the bar to open the door. The other between her throat and chest.

"Harper."

She looked up. The light over the door illuminated her and he could see bruising along her neck, and the distinct marks where fingers had dug into her skin. A blood-soaked rag hung from the hand on the door, which she now dashed through.

"No, no, no, no." He sprang down the steps, taking two or three at a time and almost wiping out on the landing. When he burst through the door, he got tangled with two couples on the sidewalk.

He pushed them out of the way. "Sorry."

Harper was dodging cars on the boulevard. From somewhere, a shot rang out, and pedestrians began to scream and run toward the garage, seeking cover. He moved around people to keep her in his line of vision, while also scanning the area for a shooter.

The shot sounded like it came from a higher position. *From one of the casino balconies?*

No way of telling for sure. He knew sound could be distorted in a situation like this, and it could have come from almost any direction. All these distractions gave Harper enough time to slip into a taxi, which then melted into traffic.

Having lost her, he again turned to search out the shooter, but saw only partiers and policemen who, having heard the gunfire, were pouring out of the garage with their guns drawn. Cash bent over, his hands on his knees, sucking in air.

"Did you catch her?"

Not changing his position, he twisted his head to stare at Ian. He held up a hand but couldn't speak yet.

"I know. I know. You're gonna kick my ass, right?"

Cash nodded rapidly, gulping. Moving his hands to his back, he straightened. After a few minutes, when his breathing came down to the level of a marathoner breaking through the tape, he stumbled toward the entrance to the garage. Ian didn't speak, but began whistling the theme song from *Rocky*. He never wanted to beat someone so badly, and been so incapable of doing it.

Unless it was that bastard Lewis DePesto. That hulking monster choked her. He was four times her size. Cash ground his teeth as he reentered the crime scene. An officer was repairing the tape where he'd broke through it. He looked over at Cash, scowling at him.

"Sorry about that."

Cash made his way over to the lead detective. Beason grinned when he looked up at him and abruptly ended his conversation with a junior detective. Before he could open his mouth, Cash muttered, "Don't start." His glare must have spoken volumes because Beason backed down.

"What do you have so far?"

He hesitated, tapping his pen on the edge of his notebook and working his jaw. He looked back and forth between Ian and Cash. After a few seconds, he sighed and looked at his scribbling. "Victim was a Kitty Carmichael from St. Louis, Missouri. She's worked at the casino for about five years. Manager said she was involved in drugs."

Cash raised his eyebrows. That didn't sound like somebody Harper would hang out with. Although, what did he really know about Harper. He called to Mitzi, "See any signs of drug abuse?"

37

"No tracks on her arms, if that's what you mean. And hair and teeth are too pretty to be a meth user."

He jerked his head in acknowledgement. "Thanks." Returning his attention to the detective, he asked, "What else do you have?"

"That's all I got. Got here myself fifteen minute ago," he huffed, crossing his arms. "What's your interest anyway?"

"What do you mean?"

He nodded to the upper level of the garage. "Who's the girl?"

Cash looked at Ian, debating over whether to tell Beason. Ian studied the man, frowning at him for a moment, but looked at Cash and shrugged.

Maybe if I give him a little info, he'll share more with me.

He glanced around to see if anyone was near enough to hear. He and Ian drew Beason a few more feet away. "We believe she witnessed the shooting."

He whistled—which Cash found annoying—then seemed to take the information in. "Uh-uh. There's more." He pointed again to the area where they spotted Harper. "Why were you willing to risk your neck to get her?"

He glanced at Ian and shrugged. "I was the last person to see her before she went on the run. I guess I feel responsible for her."

"Plus, she's cute."

Cash made a move toward his partner, who ducked behind the detective's back. "You know what…?"

Ian peeked from around Beason's opposite shoulder. "Ooh. Touchy, touchy."

Beason interrupted. "What's the witness's name?"

"Harper." He still glared at Ian. "I don't know her last name."

Beason lifted his shoulders. "At least it's not Mary or Jane." He scratched something down.

Cash placed a hand on his hip, thinking. "She's a dealer. Card dealer. Also from St. Louis."

"How did you meet her?"

Ian came out from behind his shield.

"I was doing some surveillance." Cash shifted his feet. "Playing at her table. We talked a little. Oh, her last name is Collins. Harper Collins."

Beason raised his eyebrows and shook his head, but made a notation.

"I think a floor supervisor named Lewis DePesto may somehow be involved."

He nodded. "Okay. We'll check him out."

"Do you think you can get me a picture of her?"

"The witness or the vic?"

"The witness. That was her they were taking a shot at out there."

"I'll check the employment files. What time did you talk to her?"

"Uhh…I was at her table from about seven to nine."

"Okay. Maybe we can pull the camera shots."

Cash held out his hand. "Thanks, Mike."

He shook it, but went back to his notes.

Cash tilted his head toward the entrance. "We're going back to the house and do a little checking ourselves. You know where to get me."

"Yeah, sure," he mumbled, not looking up.

Ian followed Cash out to the car.

Before getting behind the wheel, Cash looked at Ian over the roof of the Mustang. "You know what gets me? Why did she come back here? Her head is gushing like a geyser, she knows her friend's killers may still be around. Why come back?"

"Well, she's probably not thinking all that logically right now. She watched someone murder her friend then got roughed up. A bit much to take in, don't ya think?"

"True." Cash swung behind the wheel and turned to Ian once he was in. "Well, if she's not thinking logically, we have to do it for her. We're racing now. Either we find her, or they do."

His partner nodded. Serious for the first time all day.

CHAPTER FOUR

Harper stumbled into the emergency room. She was light-headed. Whether from blood loss or lack of oxygen to her brain, she didn't know. She kept the bar towel pressed against her head, but the bleeding wouldn't stop. With her free hand, she felt along the wall, using it to support herself at times.

"Help me." She kept stumbling forward. She had to get help. "Help me," she tried to say louder. Finally, a girl at the nurse's station a few yards away looked up and noticed her.

"Dr. Billings," she said to the man in scrubs looking over a chart on the opposite side of the desk.

He turned to look and they both ran toward her. She suddenly felt nauseous and even weaker than before. They reached her and were asking her questions, but everything seemed distorted. The sound faded in and out, like a radio station that couldn't quite be tuned in. Her legs buckled, and she fell to her knees. As she pitched forward, they grabbed her arms and helped her to her feet. Someone came up from behind with a wheelchair and they eased her into it.

A half hour later, after she'd had some broth, she was feeling almost normal. Except for the pounding headache and sore throat. The doctor sat on a rolling stool while she was perched on the edge of an exam table under bright lights. He was brushing her hair back, checking out his handiwork.

41

"Thirty-seven stitches." He stopped examining it and looked her straight in the eye. "That was a nasty wound." He took hold of her chin gently and swiveled her head from side to side, studying her neck. "And this is some pretty serious bruising. Who did this to you, honey? Was it your boyfriend?"

Harper thought it strange he called her honey when he wasn't that much older than her. Maybe in his early thirties. She was about to tell him, no, it wasn't her boyfriend, it was Lewis the floor supervisor from La Bonne Chance, when a man burst in. Despite having seen him through the window in the door, she jumped, or flinched, she wasn't quite sure what to call it. A uniformed policeman stood there. He was older than both her and the doctor, probably in his forties, with dark, curly hair under his hat. Tall, but of average weight. He had the radio, the gun, cuffs and everything… but something was off. Something in his eyes when he saw her through the door's window. They were cold and dead, his mouth drawn in a straight line. Then his features morphed into something else when he entered the room. Serious still, but courteous, his eyes more animated.

"If you're done there, doc, I need to take her down to the station."

A ball of ice formed in the pit of her stomach. She clutched at the doctor's arm. "No." And she knew. "He's not a cop."

The doctor stared at her, his mouth hanging open.

The policeman put his hands on his waist. "Now, Ms. Collins. It's not nice to lie to the good doctor." His patronizing tone held an edge.

The doctor slowly rose to his feet. "May I see your badge, Officer?"

"Of course." He handed the badge over and the doctor checked it out. He looked at Harper. "Looks legit."

"See now? Let's get going." He clamped onto Harper's elbow and began to drag her out of the room.

She tried to pull away. "No. They shot my friend."

The non-cop scowled at her. "She's delusional."

The doctor's jaw hardened. "Stop right there. She's my patient, and you're not taking her anywhere till I'm satisfied that is the right thing to do. Jenny." He called to a nurse, who came to the door. "Please call the police station and scc if they've sent an officer to the hospital."

Robocop continued to jerk her forward.

"Please! Help me! He's going to kill me!" Tears were spitting out of her eyes and her voice rose to hysterics. She knew she needed to stay calm, she was feeding into his story, but her nerves were shot.

"See. I think it's best if I take her on out of here. Before she hurts somebody." He changed positions, getting behind her more to push her out in front of him, while maintaining his hold.

The doctor grabbed her arm. "If she has mental issues, she will be evaluated before being released to your custody."

They stared at each other for a long moment; then the man shoved her forward. The doctor kept pace. "Like I said. She's my patient and she's not going anywhere. Jenny! Call security."

"You shouldn't have done that."

It all happened so fast, Harper couldn't believe her eyes. The "policeman" let go of her for a second, grabbed the doctor's arm, pushed him against the doorframe, and made a slashing movement across his neck. The doctor's eyes bugged out, and he clutched at his throat, but blood seeped between his fingers. Harper shrieked, tears running down her face, and tried to catch him as he crumbled to the ground.

Nurses were shouting and running away, although one seemed frozen, like her, horrified by the blood now pooling on the floor. "Dr. Billings!" she finally forced out. She moved forward and caught his arm.

Harper was shaking uncontrollably. She looked at the nurse. "What do we do? What do we do?"

She was wrenched away from his side by her

abductor. "We're getting out of here."

She was vaguely aware of being dragged down the hall. She couldn't take her eyes off the doctor. The nurse got him on his back and was pressing her hands to the cut, but she was covered in his blood.

"Come on. Come on."

A searing sensation sizzled up her arm as he yanked her along. She strained against him, even though it increased her pain.

Her captor bent to throw her over his shoulder, and a male nurse jumped out of a doorway, hitting him over the head with a metal bedpan. It rang out like a gong. It would have been comical if a man weren't bleeding out mere feet away from her. The policeman straightened, letting go of her briefly. Without hesitation, he threw a roundhouse punch to the nurse's jaw. He went down and was absolutely still.

A second male nurse jumped out of the room, smaller in size and stature than the first. His eyes were round as he held his fists up awkwardly, but he turned his head to her and said, "Run! Run!"

She turned and stumbled forward a couple of feet, then caught her footing and ran.

"Shit!" a male voice cried out. The heavy *thuds* of punching came from behind her and a crash of a body hitting the wall, but she kept forcing her feet forward.

"Shit!" came again, but from a different male voice, the policeman's. She didn't stop to look if he was following her, just flew. Sirens near the ceiling went off, lights flashing, and a voice came over the intercom.

"Security alert in the emergency department. Patients and staff are advised to stay in their rooms. Remain out of the hallways, and bar your doors, if possible." The voice was way too calm.

She ran down so many halls, around so many corners, seeing no one, until she was hopelessly lost. She sobbed, remembering the doctor's face. He was only trying to help her. Her chest hurt, ached as she struggled to breathe. She

looked back as she neared a corner and plowed into
something. It was so jarring her mind hadn't quite caught up
with what happened, but as they separated she saw the
uniform. When she lifted her head, she was shocked to find a
different man in police garb staring at her with an evil smile.
Visclike hands gripped her arms.

"Gotcha." He released her with one hand, pulled his
arm back, gritted his teeth, and she saw his fist coming,
then…nothing.

***

She opened her eyes and groaned. Everything hurt,
but most especially, the side of her head. Voices surrounded
her, they were shouting but she couldn't make out what they
were saying. She used all of her strength to push her upper
body away from the cold, white floor.

Where am I?

Her head hung uselessly. She couldn't lift it. Then
hands were locking around her arms. She fought her head up
enough to see the legs, which were uniformed. With effort,
her gaze climbed to the waist, where a holster hung from a
belt. She let them lift her, but when her feet hit the ground,
she launched her body away from them. Surprisingly, she
was released. She struggled forward and stumbled, but threw
an arm out and was able to steady herself on a wall. They
shouted, but she couldn't hear. Her ears were ringing. She
could see the warning lights by the ceiling still circling, the
sirens screeching. She kept moving. She had to move.

She felt her way around the corner, and it appeared
before her. A door to the outside. Her heart leapt. She looked
from side to side warily but no one was in the hall running
perpendicular to hers, that she could see. The door became
the only thing that existed, like a swimmer fighting their way
to the surface, almost out of air. She didn't take her eyes
from it.

When she reached it, it magically slid open. Chilly

night air hit her, but she'd never felt anything so good. Her progress was painfully slow. She had nothing left. And where was she to go, exactly? She made it around the corner of the brick building, but she could see people milling about. Her heart raced. Were they people who could help her? Or hurt her? She couldn't take a chance. She whirled around, heading in the opposite direction and wrapping her arms around herself. The wind now chilled her. She'd left her coat in the break room. But that was a lifetime ago. Louder voices reached her. People were close. True panic seized her. She managed to pick up her pace and came upon a wide area that looked like a loading dock.

Where? Where can I be safe?

She spotted a dumpster and her mind focused on it. *The dumpster.*

Next to it was a concrete platform. Four metal rungs seemed to grow out of the wall. Reaching it, she put her foot on the bottom rung but forgot how to climb for a moment. When she placed her hands on the higher bars, the cold metal bit into her. She gritted her teeth. Normally she would have drawn back. But that sort of pain was of no consequence now. She worked her other foot onto the ladder. It seemed to take forever. She eyed her path.

Four little rungs. I can do this. I have to.

When she pulled herself up, pain shot along her arm to her shoulder and she cried out. She blinked, and in a flash and she saw Kitty falling, gun shots ringing out, sounding so real it was almost like she was back there. She jerked her head but another vision claimed her. The doctor. They came for her. He only tried to help her. Tears tracked their way down her face and she sobbed softly, but she coaxed the weight of her body upward, despite the excruciating pain. Once at the top, she crawled out onto the concrete and flopped on the ground. This wasn't part of the plan. So cold. So tired. So numb. She cried, huge sobs wracking her body, already sore from all she'd been through. She thought of giving up. Just lying there until they came to kill her.

Momma, I'm sorry. Daddy…

She didn't know how long she'd been curled up on the platform when a horn honking somewhere stirred her. With effort, she moved her head, searching. A pole jutted out of the concrete a few feet away and she let her gaze follow it. A light higher up blared, blinding her, so she threw an arm up to block it. A yellow box sat on top of the post with two huge buttons. One green. One red. Her mind processed all this slowly. She dragged herself over, using the solid metal almost like a rope, and worked her way to her feet. She surveyed the area, forgetting her purpose until she sighted the dumpster. It took everything she had in her to lift the lid enough to slide under it. She tumbled down, unable to control her fall, but the landing wasn't painful.

It was warmer now but smelled. The absolute dark scared her, but she couldn't do anything about it. The plastic bags were somehow comforting. She was safe, for now. She let go, and drifted away.

CHAPTER FIVE

Cash was barely in the squad room before he called out. "What do you have, Jerry?"

"A pay phone. I didn't even know they still had those things. About three blocks from here."

"In which direction?"

"Hold on." He typed into his computer. Hunting and pecking, but impressively fast. "It's at Fourth and Division. West."

"Between here and the casino," Ian pointed out.

Cash nodded. "She's sticking close. Places that are familiar to her."

Jerry spoke up. "I've got her home address, too."

Their heads spun. "Really?" they both said at the same time.

"But, you didn't even know her name. How did you find—"

Ian interrupted. "We couldn't find anything for her online."

"Beason." When they continued to stare at him, Jerry added, "I knew he caught the case. Thought he could help. He got the info off her employment records." He held up a slip of paper.

Cash snatched it. "Put some men outside her place, and—"

"I've already done it." Mike Beason strode up behind

them. He gave them a hard stare.

"Oh, yeah. He's here," Jerry said belatedly. The phone rang, and he picked it up.

"Whose case is this anyway, Delmonaco?"

Cash held up his hands. "Yours, Mike. Yours."

"Good. Then you need to check with me before you do anything." He studied him, hesitating. "I was coming to bring you this." From a file folder, he withdrew a picture, handing it over.

She can even make an employment picture look good.

Beason leaned in. "I can see why you're so hot to do her now."

I am not hot to "do" her. What is wrong with everybody? Although…I wouldn't exactly object…

Cash opened his arms wide, looking around the room. "Has everyone forgotten we're talking about a murder witness here?" Most of the other officers were busy on their phones or messing with paperwork, and, in any case, didn't know what he was talking about. They gave him a quizzical look but continued going about their business. Beason gave him a wry smile, dipped his head and left.

Ian yawned. Cash patted him on the back. "I know it's late, buddy. And you're way over your shift. We can't do any productive canvassing, most of the shops will be closed. But we'll start showing her picture around downtown tomorrow." He checked his phone. "It's even too late to call her parents, although it's eleven their time… You should go on home and get some shut eye."

"What are you going to do?"

Cash rubbed the back of his neck. "I don't know. Walk around downtown and look for her, I guess."

"Then I'm going with you."

"Are you sure? It's likely a wild goose chase. And I'm sure Beason has some cars down there on the lookout anyway."

"No. I'm going. I want to find her, too."

"Okay. If you're—"

Jerry interrupted. "Cash, a girl fitting your description was attacked at Victory Medical Center."

A chill crept over his skin. "Was she hurt?"

"No. But she ran off. Doctor was seriously injured trying to defend her, though. He's in surgery right now. They don't know if he'll make it. Guy was dressed like a cop, and security ran off a second attacker who was also dressed as a cop."

But she's okay.

Relief swept through him so fast he almost felt sick.

"Great. Now she won't trust the cops. We've hung up on her—sorry, Jerry—and attacked her," Ian pointed out.

Cash's shoulders slumped. "Our job got a lot harder."

***

Harper woke gagging. The stench was too much. In the darkness, she thought for a moment maybe she was buried alive. But the plastic she was laying on reminded her she hid in a dumpster. Groaning, she rolled over and could see the slim crack of light from the outside. She stood awkwardly, trying to balance on the unstable surface. Cracking the dumpster open, and not seeing anyone, she attempted to get out. With her arm still sore, she wasn't quite able to pull herself up. She rummaged around and stacked bags on top of bags to give her a boost. One of the bags leaked on her hand. She didn't want to think about what kind of fluid might be in a hospital dumpster. She wiped her hands on her uniform and gripped the rim of the dumpster, climbing her makeshift stepladder. She was able to make it out, albeit not gracefully, but luckily no one was in the vicinity to catch it.

She brushed herself off and looked around. The loading area she stood in was empty now, but would surely be coming to life soon.

Now what?

She obviously couldn't call the cops. She couldn't go

home. They'd be watching there. And she couldn't exactly roam the streets. She'd be an open target. A breeze stirred and she got a whiff of something unpleasant. Herself.

Well, first off, I need to get out of these clothes. I can find a bathroom and at least clean up some. And then I'll have to do something with this hair. The red will be a beacon for them.

She decided going back into the hospital to try to find scrubs would be too risky. They had cameras and would probably be on high alert after last night. She really wanted to find out how the doctor was doing. She reassured herself he was in the best possible place and received treatment almost immediately. He was alive. That had to be true. One thing was for certain, she wasn't letting anyone else get hurt. She'd involve no one.

Somehow, she needed to get out of this city. The keys to her car and her purse were in her locker at the casino. Kitty's hurrying her had made her flustered, and she'd left them behind. She realized now Kitty must have known someone was after her. The question remained, why?

And how.

How do I get out of this mess alive?

All she had was her tips from the previous night. If that money was still in her pocket. She checked and was relieved to find it was. She didn't think it would be enough for a bus ticket. Then again, she'd never taken a bus, so she really had no way of knowing.

What she did know was she needed to get clean clothes. Near La Bonne Chance was a secondhand store. She decided to make her way there. But, by back roads and alleyways, where they might not see her, but she'd be alone if they did? Or main roads where she might be able to blend in? She decided on the latter. The streets would probably be crowded with commuters by now.

But no way was she chancing walking across the huge parking lot. She'd be like those targets at the county fair guys threw baseballs at. Only these guys wouldn't be throwing baseballs. And they wouldn't miss.

They have to be watching the hospital, knowing I probably didn't get far.

She stared at her only other option. A twelve-foot chain link fence.

Ugh. Why does everything have to involve climbing?

She rubbed her shoulder in preparation, staring at the fence like an enemy. Then, deciding there was no better time than the present, she latched on, took a deep breath, and began to climb. Her tattered hose immediately caused her problems, getting hooked on the wires. She stepped back off and removed what remained of her hose, which hurt like crazy. Fibers were stuck to the cuts on her feet, actually imbedded in places, and ripping them off meant opening wounds again.

Once she got started, up didn't bother her nearly as much as down. She didn't know if that was because it was a different movement, or if the sore arm was just tired at that point. The bare feet didn't help much either. She never realized how much stress her shoes took in certain situations until she didn't have them. She would surely face some stares on the street.

It was terrifying walking out of the tree line surrounding parts of the hospital and reaching the street. This street was only moderately traveled, with several car repair shops and warehouses. There were so many hiding places for anyone trying to find her. Behind stacks of tires, or dilapidated cars. In doorways, in the cars on the street... When she reached a cross road she breathed a sigh of relief.

One more block and I'll be on Victory.

This block was shorter, but equally scary. She saw only one other pedestrian, on the opposite side of the street. The way he was gawking at her made her nervous, but she thought again that someone in a wrinkled, black La Bonne Chance dealer dress, walking without shoes, might give one a reason to wonder. Plus, her hair had to be wacked. She tried to pat it down. She'd need to buy a comb, too.

Victory was humming with life, a steady stream of people on both sides of the street going to their jobs. As she approached one couple, the guy's nose wrinkled.

"Ooh. What the hell is that?"

"Probably the sewers," his companion guessed. "Man. That is awful."

Several yards beyond them a man dressed as a rabbi passed her then came running back to tap her on the shoulder. She jumped and spun around. He held up his hands.

"I didn't mean to scare you, miss. I was wondering, are you okay?"

"What?"

He hesitantly pointed to his forehead. She caught her reflection in a shop window. She'd lost her bandage somewhere and maybe ripped a few stitches as the cut was bleeding again.

Great. As if I don't already look like a huge freak.

"I'm fine. Thank you. I have to go."

She whirled around and walked faster. She heard him from behind her.

"Are you sure?"

She didn't bother to answer, but was so distracted she bumped her shoulder against some woman, whose friend snapped at her.

"Why don't you watch where you're going?"

"Leave her alone," the woman she ran into hissed.

Pedestrians stared and whispered to one another. If they thought they were being subtle, they were dead wrong. Noses wrinkled. People fanned the air in front of them when she got near. A big man with a white T, suspenders, jeans, and a hard hat, was walking her way, still several feet in front of her. His gaze focused on her and Harper's heart rate accelerated. His expression was blank, eyebrows scrunched together. He stuck a hand in his pocket, and she felt sure he was going to pull a gun out. She thought about running, but he was upon her too quickly.

He passed by without incident. She squeezed her eyes

shut and inhaled deeply. She realized she'd held her breath as he approached. On the other side of Victory was the thrift shop she needed. But no one was waiting there, and she didn't dare cross alone, out in the open. And, anyway, it looked closed. Ahead, a neighborhood pharmacy sat on the corner, its lights beaming OPEN. She hustled to keep pace with the others crossing the street and ducked inside.

I can get hair color here and at least take care of that.

The first aisle she turned up had T-shirts with the outline of New York State on them, "Victory is the place to be!" was the claim in the middle.

Yes! Maybe I won't have to go to the thrift store.

She grabbed a shirt from the front, which happened to be pink with white lettering. But there were no sweat pants. What good was the T without pants?

Maybe in another aisle?

Holding onto hope, she moved over an aisle and found hair color. She studied the shelves, found the cheapest brand, and plucked one off. She sighed.

I always wondered what it would be like to be a blonde. Funny. I never thought it could save my life before now.

She felt eyes on her and looked over. Two pharmacists had their heads together talking, looking at her.

Probably think I'm shoplifting.

Ignoring them, she found an inexpensive comb on the other side of the aisle, then went to put the T-shirt back.

I guess I do need to go to the thrift store after all. Besides, I need shoes.

But when she went to hang the shirt up, she spotted something. Feeling all the way to the back of the row she retrieved a pair of flannel pajama pants.

Not quite my style. But I've seen other women wear these in public. It'll have to do.

When she turned, the shorter of the two pharmacists stood blocking her way. He was maybe five-five, with brown eyes and thin brown hair, and wire-rim glasses. A few years older than her, she judged.

"Can I help you, miss?" He had a fast way of talking, like he was from NYC or something.

"I was just coming to check out. I swear."

"Oh, I don't doubt that," he said kindly. "It's just—" He held a hand at about her forehead height, "I could clean that and bandage it for you."

The cut. She'd forgotten about it. Before she could protest, he snagged a first aid kit from a bottom shelf.

"Oh, I can't afford—"

"It's not a problem. We needed one behind the counter anyway. Come with me." He marched off.

She hesitated, but ended up following him. He set the kit down on the customer side of the counter and worked on opening it. The other pharmacist came over.

"Hi," he said awkwardly, one hand drumming on the counter. He was tall, and heavy, with curly hair. He also wore glasses with thick rims.

"Oh, I need to get these." She shoved her purchases onto the counter and he hesitantly began to ring her in. Spotting some thin, silky women's scarves on display, she drew one out and put it with the rest.

"Okay," the man at her side said. She turned and he held an antiseptic wipe up. "This might hurt." He placed his other hand under her chin and dabbed at the wound carefully. She didn't flinch. "Yeah. You ripped a couple of your stitches open, but it doesn't look too bad."

His friend addressed her. "Uhh…it's gonna be $21.21."

"Oh." She dug into her pocket, trying to look down while the man continued to clean her cut. She held out some bills. "I think this has got it."

He took them. "Yeah. Yeah. This is enough all right."

She heard the drawer slide open, the slap of the bars holding the money coming up, and the jingle of change. When her caretaker reached for a bandage, she turned to get her change. "Thank you." She only had like twenty-five dollars left.

The pharmacist who was taking care of her cleared his throat, and she lifted her head. He held a bandage ready and smoothed it over the stitches. "There now. That's better." He smiled and turned to snap the kit closed.

"Thank you so much."

"No problem. That's our job. To take care of people. Is there anything else we can help you with?"

"Well…you wouldn't have a bathroom, would you?"

"Of course. Right this way." Leaving the kit on the counter he led her over to the restrooms beyond the shelves.

Before he could turn to go, she put a hand on his arm. "Thank you. Thank you for your kindness."

"Oh, I'm returning the favor. Ten months ago, I was on the street, like you, and you emptied your pocketbook for me. And I've seen you do it for others, too. That money inspired me to get a suit and apply for jobs, and that's how I got this one. I should be the one thanking you." He smiled and walked away.

Harper stood for a moment with her mouth hanging open. Then she smiled for the first time in—it seemed like forever. She opened the door to the bathroom and was relieved to find the space empty. She entered a stall to change her clothes, but thought better of it and began the process of coloring her hair.

About halfway through, a woman and small child walked in. The woman inhaled, fluttering a hand to her chest.

Harper scrambled to her feet. "Sorry. I'm…well, coloring my hair."

The woman nodded, stared at her strangely, shielding her child and taking her into the bigger handicapped stall. Harper had no idea how long the color had been in, or whether it would work at all. She glimpsed in the mirror and had to do a double take. Her hair looked almost white.

"Mommy, why is that lady washing her hair here? Doesn't she have a home?"

"I don't know, sweetheart. Finish up." The mother's voice was warm, and Harper was pleased to hear some everyday conversation.

The stall cracked open and she jumped away from the sink. "Thank you," the mother said evenly. But her daughter stared up at Harper.

"I have a new church dress."

Harper smiled. "It's lovely."

"Is that your church dress?"

She didn't know what to say. "No. It's my work dress."

"Come on, Priscilla." The mother interrupted. "Let's wash your hands."

Harper caught the mom's gaze in the mirror, then looked away, her face warming.

"That's a lovely shade."

At first Harper didn't know what the woman was talking about, but she nodded in the direction of the box on the counter.

"Oh. Thank you." She moved so they could get by her.

As they passed, the mother leaned over, squinting her eyes in the dim light. "I think you're done. Your hair, I mean."

"Oh. Great. Thanks."

Harper rinsed her hair and stared at the girl in the mirror. Having never colored her hair before, she couldn't believe the transformation. Another customer came in, so she swept her mess into the trash and changed clothes. Stepping out, she wrapped the scarf around her neck to hide some of the bruising.

I look like a hillbilly Jackie O.

She allowed herself a smile.

And I thought I'd never make it on those Survivor shows. I thought I'd be gone before the first commercial break. Well, I'm still alive. And I'm gonna keep it that way.

A big pair of glasses would hide her face more, but

she needed to save her money. Who knew how long she'd be without access to cash? She was more than happy to throw her stinky dress in the trash. Besides, it reminded her of Kitty. About to walk out the door, she paused. She took a few steps back and pushed all evidence of her being there under the other trash.

When she walked out, the smaller pharmacist was handing a customer a package with a smile. The larger one gawked at her, then elbowed his friend, who blinked.

"Hi. Wow. That's quite a difference. If I passed you on the street, I wouldn't recognize you."

Perfect.

She knew she should keep moving. Staying in one place probably wasn't wise. "Well, thank you, again, for your help."

"Oh. Wait." He got something from under the counter, then came out through the swinging half door with a bag. He stuck his hand inside it. "Here's these." He handed her a pair of orthopedic socks. "Not real attractive, but they'll keep you warm."

"But I don't—"

"It's on me. Annnd this." He slapped a Victory hat on her head. White and pink like her shirt. She laughed. "We don't sell any footwear, but I have these. They're guys, so they'll be way too big for you, but at least it's something."

"But—"

"It's an old pair anyway. I just wear 'em to walk here, then I slip into these babies." He stuck out his work shoes. "A Mister Roger's kind of thing."

Harper hesitated. "Okay. But only across the street. Then I'll bring them right back."

"Charlie's Thrift Emporium? Great idea. And if they don't have any shoes, keep mine for as long as you need them."

"Well, Dave—" She'd read his name on his coat. "—thank you so much. You're an angel." She bent and kissed him on the cheek.

"What about me?" the bigger guy behind the counter asked. "I found the support hose."

"And thank you—" She leaned to one side to read the name on his coat. "—Frank."

"What? No kiss?"

Dave waved him off. "Bah." He handed her a business card. "Here's my number if you need a place to stay. My wife and I would be happy to have you."

"My number's on the back, too. And I don't have no wife to get in the way, blondie."

Dave turned the card over and whirled around, throwing up his hands. "Are you kidding me? When did you do that?"

He smiled and shrugged. "When you were helping that lady."

Dave turned back to Harper, red in the face. "Do NOT. Do NOT call that man. That would be the worst mistake you made in your life."

"Hey. I consider that mildly offensive."

"Shut up, would ya?"

"Fine!"

Dave walked her over to the door. "Good luck. And I mean it. Don't call him. For your own good." He let the door shut, but not before Harper heard him mumble, "Sleeping in a damn dumpster would be better than that."

"I doubt it." She twisted her head to look back. Frank blew her a kiss. "Then again…"

CHAPTER SIX

The real person who needed to be arrested was the person who made the coffee at the station. Or the bilge water they tried to pass off as coffee. Cash set his Buffalo Bills mug on the break table, then leaned on the back of a chair with one hand, the other rubbing his eyes, which burned like hellfire. Or what he imagined hellfire would feel like.

"You look like shit." Ian always came straight to the point. No beating around the bush for him. "Did you sleep in that?"

Cash looked at his outfit. "Maybe."

Ian crossed to pull his own Patriots cup down, and tipped the coffee pot over it. "Did you sleep at all?"

He grunted as a response.

Sleep. How could I sleep knowing she was out there? Somewhere. Probably being shot at. All alone.

He was a cop. He was supposed to protect people. He was as useless now as he was when he was twelve and the mugger kindly spared him, while leaving his parents' corpses on the cold ground. He had to do something to find her.

"Do you think it's too early to call her parents? Seven o'clock their time."

"Nah. They're probably up by seven."

They strolled into the squad room but didn't even get the chance to sit before their captain stuck his head out of his office door.

"Delmanaco. Tate."

Cash and Ian exchanged a look.

Ian nudged him. "He looks pissed."

Captain William Fitzgerald—or as the fellas liked to call him when he wasn't around, Wee Little Willie—was wearing that stern father look that struck every member of the squad with fear. He could lecture an officer into the grave.

They crossed the room, shoulder to shoulder. Cash spoke out of the corner of his mouth, keeping his eye on the captain. "Shit. Did you fill him in?"

Ian turned his head. "No. Did you?"

Cash couldn't answer, because they were at the doorway where the captain stood back to let them pass. To his left, someone rose. Their view had been blocked by a set of filing cabinets, so Cash wasn't prepared.

"Cash. Ian." Dr. Chiyo Hayashi shook their hands.

Cash nodded because he'd lost his voice. Chiyo was the precinct's shrink. He seemed to know everything. Look into your soul. And Cash didn't like having his soul looked at. Chiyo barely passed him on his initial psych exam, because he somehow found out about Cash watching his parents bleed to death in a parking lot after a mugging turned nasty. Chiyo questioned this as his motivation for joining the force. In the end, Cash must have answered something that satisfied the doctor, and he passed.

Captain Fitzgerald strolled around to the other side of the room, leaned forward a moment, arms outspread, the fingertips of both hands resting on his desk, then slowly lowered himself into his chair.

"So I understand you boys are helping homicide with a case. How do I understand that? Because Captain Rick Stout called me. Of course, I had no idea what he was talking about…"

Ouch. The disappointed look.

Chiyo watched things with his usual, aggravating

calm. His gaze slid around to each player as he leaned back in the only comfortable chair in the office, his fingers steepled in that disturbing way he had.

Cash held his palms up, arms wide. "Cap, we just got back. I didn't even sit yet."

"I know, but fellas, here's the thing, they have these things called radios in most police cars now. And I'm certain you both have a cell phone...?" He raised his eyebrows, looking from one to the other.

They glanced at each other then back at him, nodding simultaneously. He reclined in his chair with a sigh, lacing his fingers and laying his hands on his pooch.

"Dr. Hayashi here—" He nodded in the psychiatrist's direction. "—has been assigned to the case. As a profiler. To help us determine what our witness's next move might be. He—and *I*—would like to know everything you know about what's going on at La Bonne Chance."

Cash looked over at Chiyo, who was penetrating him with his laser-vision eyes. The office, which was small, and always crowded with stuff—case files, cabinets—seemed to be getting even smaller by the second. Chiyo wore gray pants, starched so stiffly Cash thought they could probably stand in the corner by themselves. Added to that was a thin gray sweater over a pressed white shirt. Not a wrinkle to be found anywhere. *He* could use a shrink.

Definitely some potty-training issues.

Cash let it rest. What he really wondered about was the manila folder sitting in front of him on the desk, perfectly aligned with the corner. It had Harper's name on it. He needed to get a look at it. He leaned forward, hunching his shoulders slightly and placing his forearms on the chair's armrests.

"We were doing our initial surveillance as you instructed, and—"

"From the film I watched, it looked like you were mostly surveying that cute little red-headed dealer you were playing with." He snickered, looking at Chiyo.

Cash's mouth dropped open.

Film? There was film? What? Was it being passed around the squad room for everyone's entertainment?

Cash looked over at Ian, who shrugged.

A lot of help you are.

He cleared his throat and started again. "Look. I played some cards, we had like a ten-minute conversation, she—"

"Twenty-one minutes, six seconds." Dr. Hayashi sat forward and participated in the conversation for once.

"Huh?"

"The time was on the film."

"O-okay. I wasn't exactly keeping time. I was trying to play poker and watch the suspect—"

Captain Fitzgerald tilted his head. "And doing a bad job at both of them, in my opinion."

"Especially the cards," Hayashi added.

The captain nodded. "*Especially* the cards."

This is the one thing he hated about the job. The constant ribbing and posturing. It got old. Although, if he were honest with himself, he usually could take it as easy as giving it out. Maybe he *was* gaga for the girl.

It's concern. Concern and physical attraction. You can't build a relationship out of that. It was nothing.

Cash jumped to his feet and moved around to stand behind his chair, gripping the top of it. "Look. A girl's out on the street—a nice girl—and some not very nice guys are looking to kill her. So if we could cut it with all the joking around for a minute and discuss ways to keep her alive…"

Chiyo put his hands in his lap. "You're right. I apologize. Tell me everything you know about the girl. Don't leave anything out. Even the most insignificant detail can help me to get inside her head, so to speak."

Satisfied, Cash took a deep breath and returned to his seat, even turning toward Chiyo a bit. "So, we talked, she disappeared for a while and came back. I thought she'd left, but she went into the security office and that's where I think she was choked."

"Wait. Back up. You talked. What did she tell you?"

"I don't know. That her name was Harper Collins."
He smiled, remembering. "Her mama was a reader."

"Harper Collins? Like the publisher?" Captain
Fitzgerald crossed his arms over his chest, furrowing his
brow.

Cash nodded. "Exactly."

Chiyo was riveted to every word he was saying. "Go
on."

"She's from St. Louis. It said that on her nametag.
But you have her employment records, so you know all that."

He nodded. "But there's only so much you can get
from someone's name, age, and place of birth. I need to
know what she's like. Tell me more. She's from St. Louis, so
what brought her here?"

A mistake. That statement haunted him.

"Detective?" Chiyo prodded.

He didn't want to tell them anything that might
embarrass her.

"Detective, if there is something more you know that
could save the girl's life…"

Heat rose from Cash's midsection to his neck. He
tugged on his collar. "I'm telling you all I know." *All you
need to know, anyway.* "Why wouldn't I tell you all I know?"

"Out of some misdirected loyalty to the girl."

HOW did he know this shit?

For a tense moment, Chiyo sat back and stroked his
chin, trying to read him. It made Cash squirm. On the inside.
He wasn't giving him anything on the outside. The doctor
shifted. "Let's go over it again."

"Here." The captain reached for a remote, pointing it
toward a monitor in the corner Cash didn't noticed before.
"Let's watch the film. It might jog your memory."

It felt odd watching himself on video. Watching her.
Feeling Chiyo watching him.

"Narrate what's going on."

Cash sighed. "We were at the table. Talking." He saw himself look away and Harper's facial expression change, something he couldn't see before. She was pissed. Why?

I guess it is kind of rude to stare off. I was holding up play.

"We talked about our names. She thought I was giving her a fake one."

Chiyo tilted his head to the side.

"Cash. In a casino."

The psychiatrist nodded.

The video went on to show him losing. Luckily, no one said anything about that. Then Jimbo's friends got up…

"What's this guy's story?" Ian piped up.

"Douche was hitting on her."

Ian snorted.

"What about you, Tate?" the captain asked. "We saw you earlier, but you seem to disappear."

"We noticed some patterns at the bar," he explained. "Women and men pairing up, looked like they were being introduced to each other by the same man. After a brief period, they'd go to a room."

The captain nodded. "Prostitutes."

"High-end prostitutes. I followed one couple. She had the key. I hung out in the hallway for a while, and pretty quickly I could hear them going at it." He grinned, but the captain didn't seem amused. "Then some couple came along and I had to pretend to leave a room and I went downstairs," Ian finished quickly.

Chiyo seemed annoyed by the disruption. "Let's rewind. We missed a little bit." The captain rewound, and started it over. "Okay. A group leaves, but one guy stays around to proposition her. How did she handle that?"

Pretty slickly.

"First she told him she wasn't sure when she'd get off. That sometimes she had to work later than scheduled. He said he'd wait." Cash looked at Ian and rolled his eyes.

"Definite douche."

"So she told him dealers weren't allowed to fraternize with customers. He couldn't take no for an answer. Insisted he'd meet her after work, she'd be on her own time, and her employers couldn't say anything about it."

"Uh-huh."

"Then she told him she had a break at nine, but got off at ten. Only when she left for break at nine, that was actually when she got off."

Ian grinned. "Smooth!"

Dr. Hayashi also smiled. "Impressive. She's quick-witted, resourceful. That's probably the only thing that's kept her alive thus far."

They were quiet for a moment, concentrating on the video. Harper looked over at the older gentleman at the opposite corner of the table.

"She was nice to the old man," Cash said softly. The words came out without him thinking about them. He shook himself a little. On the TV, the old man hobbled over to him and leaned in.

"What about here," Chiyo said, pointing to the screen. "What was he saying here?"

Cash recalled the old man implying he should go after Harper. "Oh. I don't remember." He knew Chiyo wouldn't buy that. "He was joking around. Seemed like a character." He chanced a look up.

Chiyo's lips were tight, head turned in Cash's direction, his eyes squinting, as if he were deciphering some ancient stone tablet or something. They watched the rest of the video in silence.

Chiyo brushed at some invisible piece of lint on his slacks. "So, let's review what we know. Our witness's name is Harper Collins. She's from St. Louis. She's kind to the old man...Midwestern girl...what was she doing here?"

She said it was a mistake. Either a gambling habit, or some guy. I'd put my money on it being a guy.

Since he didn't elaborate, Chiyo started again. "She's scared. She can't turn to anyone she knows, either for fear of them being connected somehow to the killers, or fear of them being hurt by them. She's over the limit on her credit card, and her cash will run out at some point. She hasn't gone back to her apartment because she probably thinks they'll be waiting for her there, which is a good guess. She was at the crime scene. She may even be plotting to avenge her friend, in which case, she's in big trouble because these guys will show no mercy." He leaned forward, resting his arms on his thighs, his hands folded between them. "She's got to be in the area of the casino, somewhere. It's the only familiar area, besides her place, and she can blend into the crowd. That's where you should look for her."

Cash exchanged a look with Ian.

Didn't I just say that before we came in here? And I didn't need no fancy medical degree either. But I don't want to piss him off.

"Dr. Hayashi, do you think I could get a look at that file?"

Hayashi plucked it off the desk, handing it to him. "Sure. Maybe you can find something else in there to help you with your search. Make copies for yourself and get it back to me."

Pushing back his chair, Cash rose. "Captain, are we dismissed?"

"Yes. But I want to be kept in the loop on this." They were already out the door. "I mean it."

Cash opened the file, found what he needed, and crossed to his desk to jot the information down. "Could you do me a favor and copy this file then give the original to Dr. Hayashi?"

Ian took it from him. "Sure."

The phone receiver weighed heavy in Cash's hand as he stared at the base. He didn't want to alarm these people, but he needed information. He dialed the number. An eager male voice answered.

"Hello? Harper?"

Hearing her name caught Cash off guard. "No, sir.

This is Detective Cash Delmonaco of the Victory Police Department. Have you heard from Harper?"

"No. I just thought—a Victory exchange… You're calling about that low life Jared Inglebrook, aren't you? What sort of trouble is he into now?"

Cash spread his arms wide on his desk. This conversation wasn't going how he expected it to. "No, sir. I'm calling about your daughter, Harper. She—"

"Well, if she's in any trouble, you can bet Jared got her into it."

His pulse quickened. "Jared?"

"Yeah. That son-of-a-bitch took her innocence." He paused, and Cash didn't rush to fill the silence, knowing people often said more than they intended when a break in conversation felt awkward. "She was so naïve. We tried to warn her. And as if that weren't enough, he took her to that godforsaken town—please, excuse me—"

"Oh, no. It is godforsaken, at times. Especially in the winter."

"Well, he took her there and now we don't even get to see her."

Murmurs were exchanged in the background. "What was that, sir? I missed that."

"Oh, nothing. My wife was telling me to calm down is all." He took a breath. "Does Harper need bail money? How much is it? We'll pay it if she agrees to come back home."

"Uhh, no. She's not in any trouble, exactly…"

"Oh. Good. What can I do for you then, officer?"

How should I play this?

"Well, I'd be interested in you telling me a little bit more about this Jared guy…"

"Oh, I could go on all day about that one. I ask you, what does a normal thirty-six-year-old guy need with an eighteen-year-old girl?"

He wasn't sure how to answer that. "Uhh—"

"I tell you what he needs. He needs to seduce her for

his own sick reasons, take her away from anyone who might try to talk some sense into her, and steal her college savings so he can gamble with it, or spend it on some whore—ah, leave me alone, woman. You know every word I'm saying is true."

The mistake.

"What else do you need to know about the bum?"

"Uhh…nothing. You gave me quite a lot."

"Are you sure? Because I could tell you a bunch more about what that weasel did to my daughter. Do you have kids, officer?"

"No. No, not yet."

He chuckled. "A young guy, eh? Well, I hope you never know what it feels like to have your daughter call you from across the country, crying her head off because some asshole—he *is* an asshole. All right. I'll calm down." He took a deep breath. When he started again he sounded sad. "He hurt her, that's all." His voice broke. Cash wondered how to respond. "He cheated on her, lied to her, and stole from her. If there were anything else mean he could do to her, he'd have done that, too. Oh, wait. I forgot. Not only did he take every last cent she had, he ran up her credit cards. I don't know how she's surviving on that tip money of hers."

Cash closed his eyes, thinking about the paltry tips he'd given her all night.

"And if he's in any kind of trouble," he sniffed, "then nobody deserves it more."

Amen.

"Yes, sir. Well, if you could, if Harper contacts you, could you ask her to give me a call, please? We'd like to talk to her."

"Sure. Sure. Hold on, let me get some paper." He sounded tired now, all of his fury spent. Ian returned and sat at his desk across from Cash. "You find anything out?"

There was a scuffling noise, presumably of the receiver being picked up. Cash looked at Ian, but held up his hand.

"Okay. I'm ready." What's your name, Son?"

"Cash Delmonaco. D—"

"Like Johnny Cash?"

Cash rolled his eyes. "Yes. Like Johnny Cash." He spelled out his name for him and gave him the number. "Thank you very much, Mr. Collins. Say, you wouldn't happen to know anywhere else we could contact her, would you?"

"No. I'm afraid not. Wish I did."

"Well, thank you, anyway. Have a nice day, sir."

"Sorry I couldn't be of more help, officer."

"No, you were very helpful. Thank you for your time. Goodbye." He slowly put the receiver in its cradle, then let out a breath.

"Whoo!"

Ian sat forward. "What did he say?"

"Well, first and foremost, Harper hasn't contacted him, but—"

Ian waved his hands. "You gave him your number. Yeah. Yeah. What else did he say?"

"That a one," he leaned forward to read what he'd scribbled on a sticky note, "Jared Inglebrook brought her here and screwed her over royally." Cash swung out of his seat, pulling his coat off the back. "But he didn't really have any other information that could help us find her. Just several expletives to describe her boyfriend."

Ian rose and followed him out of habit.

"Are you ready to do some canvassing?"

"Yeah. Let's go find her."

CHAPTER SEVEN

Of course the casino was alive and cracking already, at almost nine o'clock in the morning. Murder didn't seem to hurt business. He looked at the marquis as he searched for a parking spot. La Bonne Chance Resort and Casino.

Yeah. You have a "good chance" of being shot if you don't watch what you're doing. Resort? More like the Hotel California. Kitty Carmichael won't be checking out, and neither will Harper, if I can't find her.

Cash pounded on his horn. "Asshole!"

"Easy buddy. It's a little old lady. She probably didn't see your blinker. A spot opened up there, anyway."

"Well, if she can't see my blinker, then she shouldn't be on the road," he mumbled. "Menace."

For all I know, Harper might have already been found, and we're waiting for Lake Erie to cough up her body.

Getting another idea, he zoomed past the empty spot.

Ian jabbed his finger on the glass of his window. "Hey. It was right there."

Cash didn't explain his change, but a few seconds later, he turned into the drive of the hospital parking lot, a little too fast, cutting into the opposite lane. A driver coming the other direction had to slam on his brakes. Cash waved his apologies and drew his Mustang up in the circle where patients were dropped off, shoving it into park, then shutting

71

off the engine.

"Ahh…last known location. Very smart."

Cash didn't comment. He was already getting out of the car.

The first nurse they showed the picture to recognize her. "That was her. The girl the police were trying to take away when Dr. Billings got hurt. I'm pulling a twelve-hour shift so I was here when it happened."

"Can you give us a description of the men pretending to be police officers?"

"Well, just the one. I didn't see the other one. But I can take you to where the security office is, and they can show you footage."

Cash gave her his most winning smile. "That would be great." When she was out of earshot, he leaned over to Ian. "Whoever she saw, it must have been someone high up in the organization for them to be going to these lengths, and trying things this risky."

Twenty minutes later, they were walking out the door Harper exited from with a security guard. Once outside, the security officer showing them around turned left. "Like I said, my men were taking on that 'cop,' and me and Tommy—he's a nurse—helped her off the floor, trying to see if she was hurt. But the moment she was up, she started thrashing around like a cat in a bathtub. We were afraid she'd hurt herself, so we let her go. Then the guy got free from Jimmy and practically ran us over on his way out."

She came this way. What would she be thinking? She'd be scared witless…

They came to the corner of the building.

"And that, gentlemen, is all I have for you. Security cameras show her leaving the building and turning left, but beyond the doorway they can't pick up much."

Cash pointed about halfway up the near side of the L-shaped hospital. "Is that the door the other guy came out of?"

"Yes."

There would have been a lot of commotion in that

direction. And the parking lot is too wide open. She'd feel exposed.

"What's in the opposite direction?" Cash turned around and they started retracing their steps.

"Not much. See where it looks like the building ends?"

They nodded.

"It actually indents there. But beyond that, it's just our loading dock, the place where we dump our trash…and that's about it. Oh, and our backup generator."

"Mind if we head there and look around?"

"No. Of course not."

When they got to the place where the building turned, a large loading dock spread out in front of them. It was a very isolated area near the property's edge. It seemed pretty dirty for a hospital—lots of chunks of black asphalt, along with the potholes they came out of, broken glass, a beer can or two... As they turned to head back he spotted something.

"Hold on."

At the edge of the concrete, where it met a foot or two of grass and a chain link fence, he picked up something that looked like a snake's skin.

"What's that?" the security guard asked.

"What's left of her hose. She was here, and probably climbed that fence to get away."

"Cash." Ian pointed at some black fibers still stuck to some of the sharper edges of the fence. "I think you're right."

Cash knew a rundown industrial area lay beyond the fence. He answered a few calls there when he was a rookie. Kids trespassing for the most part.

"Thank you for your time."

"Sure. Sure. Anytime, Officers."

Two hours, and a gazillion stores, massage parlors, adult bookstores, and the odd gas station later, Cash's feet hurt, he was dead tired, and no closer to finding Harper.

"I don't know, Ian. No one has seen her. Maybe they

73

got her, or maybe she made it out of town...."

"Why don't we try Charlie's Thrift Emporium. He's always good for a laugh."

Cash looked over at the jumble of sale signs on the window, some hanging at a diagonal, having come lose over time. "Sure."

"Officers." Charlie, a rotund fellow in striped, flowing pants, a T-shirt with a band's name on it, and a suede vest with fringes hanging down, opened his arms in greeting.

Ian stopped pretending to be looking at a rack of caftans. "Shh. How many times do we have to tell you we're undercover, man?"

He did jazz hands. "Oh, sar-rey. What can I do for you fine gentlemen? Show you some manzierres?"

Cash planted his elbows on the glass countertop and waved the picture—which had started to get a bit worn—in front of his face.

"Seen this redhead?"

"'Fraid not." He swiped a cardboard box from off the floor and turned toward a door at the back of the store.

Cash twisted his body, one elbow still on the glass and slouched, letting the counter support him. "You'd think someone with their head split open would stick out."

Ian folded his hands, placing them on top of a circular rack, one foot on the bottom rung. "I thought for sure Charlie would have a bead on this."

"Wait." Charlie spun around and slammed the box on the counter, making Cash jump. "Did you say she hurt her head? Let me see that picture."

Cash looked at Ian, raised his shoulders, then turned and showed the photo again.

"Yeah. She's been in here. Shoulda told me she dyed her hair."

Cash straightened and Ian rushed over. "Are you sure, Charlie?"

"Yeah. She had blond hair and was wearing a Victory ball cap. Looked kind of cute on her. That's her all right. Had a big bandage on her forehead. About here." He pointed to his thinning hairline.

"Did she look okay?"

"Was her neck bruised?" they both spoke at once.

"Yeah," he said to Cash. Then he told Ian. "Hard saying. She was wearing a scarf around it."

"What time do you think that was?" Cash took lead.

"It was early. She kinda popped out at me as I was putting my keys in the door. Before I even opened."

Again, they spoke at the same time.

"What was she wearing?"

"Did she buy anything?"

"Do ya mind?" Cash scowled at Ian.

Ian threw up his hands and walked away, but remained within listening range.

"What do you remember?"

Charlie rubbed the stubble on his chin. "She was wearing a T-shirt that matched the cap. Had on...I don't know...like, pajama pants?"

"Good." Cash twisted his head to look at Ian. "Did she buy anything?"

"Hey. That was my question."

"Just a pair of tennis shoes." Charlie chuckled. "Had on this giant pair of shoes. She could hardly walk in them."

Cash slapped his card on the counter. "If you hear anything..."

"I'll call you."

Cash gestured to Ian, heading toward the door. "Good. Thanks, Charlie. I owe you for that one."

"You always say that. Hey. What about those other two cops? They didn't leave me no card."

Cash and Ian froze then turned to come back. "What two cops?"

The description he gave matched the two guys who'd attacked Harper at the hospital.

"What did you tell them?"

"Nothin'. I didn't like their attitudes. Are they new?"

"They aren't cops, Charlie. They are the guys after our girl. If they come back, you tell them nothing. Got it? NOTHING. And you try to stall them and call me."

Bells above the door jingled, and an older lady walked in.

"I've got it. I've got it. You guys get out of here. I've got paying customers now."

They stepped out on the sidewalk.

"*Our* girl?"

Cash's muscles tightened. "What? It's just an expression."

"Um-hum."

He deciding ignoring his partner was the best bet. He stared across the street. "She had to get hair color somewhere..."

"It's a shame she had to color it," Ian commented as they crossed to the drugstore.

"But smart." He'd underestimated her.

When he saw the Victory T-shirts he knew they were in the right place. The pharmacists filled them in.

"Has anyone else been in asking questions about her?"

"Yeah," Frank said from behind the counter.

Dave nodded. "Two policemen."

Why are they always one step ahead of us?

"Did you tell them anything?"

"Yes. Everything we told you. Why?" He read their faces and his drained of color. "They're the guys. They're the guys who worked her over."

"Yeah." Then Cash remembered Louis. "Some of them, anyway."

"I thought it was a boyfriend. She's in really big trouble, isn't she?"

They both nodded.

"These aren't nice guys," Ian added.

Dave took a step forward. "I told them everything I told you. But what I didn't tell them was," he looked at Cash then at Ian, "she took a taxi when she left here."

Ian looked at Cash. "Going to her place?" he ventured.

Cash shrugged. "As good a guess as any." He shook Dave's hand. "Thank you." He drew a card out of his pocket. "She may come back here. Right now, you may be the only person she trusts. If she does, would you call me right away?"

He nodded.

As the three of them walked to the door, Frank hollered, "If you find Blondie, tell her I want to—"

"Shut up, Frank!" Dave opened the door for them. "Ignore him. He's a moron."

As Ian passed, Dave put a hand on his arm. "You're gonna find her, right? She's a nice lady."

"We're gonna find her," Cash assured him.

CHAPTER EIGHT

"*This* is where she lives?"

They were parked in front of an old motel converted into apartments. It had a seventies kind of feel to it, as in both built in the seventies, and inhabited by seventy-year-olds. The trim was a dingy white, and the walls a sort of tealish color, maybe. Maybe more green. It was hard to tell.

They got out of the car. "Her dad did say she was sort of short on cash. She roomed with the vic." Ian nodded and they walked slowly forward, like gunslingers in a shootout. Cash had seen prisons that looked more welcoming. He kicked a PBR can out of the street. Ian stepped over a puddle. It hadn't rained for days. Cash did not want to know who, or what, made that puddle.

They walked through an opening on the first floor, the upper floor providing a roof above them, and entered a central courtyard. It looked equally neglected. Patches of grass stood out here and there, along with weeds, some several feet tall. But it was mostly mud, and discarded children's toys. Along with a few trash bags, where the flies were having a party.

"Which way?"

Cash looked at the slip of paper Jerry handed him. "Two-O-one, so I guess…up?"

A set of stairs rose on each side of them. Ian eyed

them skeptically. "Do you think they'll hold us?" He started up.

"Step on the outsides. There's more support." Cash gave one last look around, then followed. "Hey. Did you see any uniforms out there? Or unmarked cars? Beason said he had men stationed here."

Ian didn't answer because they reached the top and two-O-one was right in front of them. The doorjamb was cracked and splintered, the chain meant as an extra deterrent hanging idly inside the opening. They drew their guns and took positions on either side of the door, which was metal and had a large dent in it. Ian nodded when he was in position, his back against the wall, one hand gripping his gun, finger on the trigger, the other below, and overlapping to hold the gun steady when, or if, he discharged his weapon. He nodded to Cash.

Cash used his booted foot to push the door open. It creaked and a piece of the frame dropped off. Both men peeked inside while still keeping mostly behind the wall. Cash looked at his partner and Ian checked the crack to make sure no one was behind the door. He nodded again. Everything was clear from his side.

"Hello?" Getting no response, he shouted, "Victory Police Department!" Again, nothing. Cash reached around and did a quick search for a light switch. He found it right away and flipped it, but the room remained murky.

She probably couldn't pay the electricity.

His heart was in his throat. Obviously someone broke in. The question remained, were they still inside, waiting for them?

He took a deep breath, pointing to himself to let Ian know he would take the lead position. On his signal, they both entered the room. They waited a moment for their eyes to adjust to the light. A small amount was coming in from a window to Cash's left, where, should someone open the tattered curtains, that person would have a beautiful view of the neighbor's door. In methodical fashion, they searched each corner of the room, relying on their training and putting faith in their hours spent at the firing range. They listened for any hint of a sound, any movement, any whisper, any breath. Cautiously they proceeded forward.

So far, so good.

When they reached the dinky kitchen on the right, Ian swung around and pointed his gun at the interior, while Cash had his back. There was nothing in the room, and nowhere to hide. Even if someone were small enough to hide in any of the cabinets, most of them were missing doors, so they'd be in plain sight. They continued moving inward until they reached a tiny bedroom on the left side. Here Cash played point, and Ian covered his back. In this room, too, a small window was cut near the top of the wall through which some light filtered. They entered, always turning to watch their back and be ready for ambush. The closet checked out, so the room was clear.

Ahead lay one more room—what Cash assumed to be a bedroom—at the end of the hall. As they crept toward it, Ian on point, Cash got a sense someone was behind him. He swung around and framed in the doorway was a figure. He could tell by the shape it was a woman, and it looked like she wore a ball cap and was approximately five foot two. Harper! In the position she was in she was a target, totally vulnerable.

He screamed out her name, which he knew he shouldn't do, and she sprinted away.

Shit.

Without thinking, he stashed his gun behind him in his waistband and took off after her. He knew Ian was retreating behind him, covering his back. When he reached the outer hallway, he listened for her footsteps, and went to the right. She was fast, but as she turned to scramble down a staircase, Cash launched himself over the railing, hitting the landing in front of her. She reversed course, rushing back up the stairwell, and turned in the wrong direction. Ian stood in front of her at about the spot Cash had jumped from. She ran to her right to escape him but he caught her where the balcony turned at a right angle. She elbowed him in the ribs so hard it knocked the wind out of him and she was able to wrestle free, although she lost her hat in the struggle. She made the top of the next staircase before Cash grabbed her arms.

She flailed and he shifted, wrapping one arm around her chest, one around her waist. She fought, the terror fueling her making it difficult to hold her. As a last resort, she tried to bite the arm wrapped around her chest but Cash anticipated her move.

"Nah-ah."

Using her own momentum, he swung her around and pushed her against the building, trapping her, his body pressed against her back. He could hear Ian wheezing to his left.

She cried out. "No! No!" Then began to shake and sob. "Please."

"Harper. Stop. It's me, Cash. *Look* at me."

He placed his hands on the wall on either side of her and gave her enough room to turn around. He moved his arm to block her when she tried to duck under it.

"Stop."

He was afraid he'd hurt her, but she wasn't giving him much of a choice but to use his strength.

"Stop. I don't want to hurt you."

Her face was contorted, twisted with rage and fear. "I knew that was a fake name," she spat. "You're working for them."

Cash tried to calm the situation, talking in a level voice. "No. I'm a cop. If you promise to be still, I'll show you my badge."

But when he went to pull it out, she squirmed, almost breaking free. Cash spun her around and pushed her against the wall. Her hand flew up, as was natural, and was over her head on the wall. He snatched her other wrist, using his weight to keep her in place, and used his free hand to force her arm down. She cried out, and he knew it hurt her, but he was surprised that hurt him. He managed to trap her wrists in one hand.

"Come on. Hold still."

"Go to hell."

He had to smile at that one. Retrieving his badge, he slapped it against the wall near her face. She looked at it, then her gaze shifted to Ian, who hobbled over, holding his badge up, too. She quieted some, so Cash released her arms and let her turn around, though he still blocked her escape. She lunged, and he forcefully returned his arm to her chest, pressing her shoulder blades against the wall.

"Like I'd believe you. They're fake."

Of course she would think that.

Cash closed his eyes for a moment. He needed to find the right words to say and he couldn't concentrate peering into those beautiful, wild eyes.

He opened them, studying her, then dropped his head and shook it.

I can't believe what I'm about to do.

He sighed. "Look." He lifted his head, his focus shifting between her eyes. "I know you're scared. I know your world has been smashed to smithereens, and the pieces will never fit back together again." He took in her pretty face, the bandage on her forehead, and the bruises now showing around her neck where the scarf fell. A new bruise burned high along her jawline. Who gave her that? His mouth went dry. "I know…those men hurt you." He had to swallow his guilt over not being there to help her, protect her from what they'd done. "But those weren't cops." He looked at Ian. "We're the good guys. The real thing."

Ian nodded.

She looked at them both, then squeezed her eyes shut, tipping her chin up. She rocked her head back and forth against the wall. "I don't know. I'm so confused." Her eyes popped open and she stared at the ceiling before slowly, and deliberately, lowering her head to look at him. Her eyes were wet, and when she blinked, a few tears leaked over the edge.

They tracked down her face, one after another. Her voice was high and full of emotion. "I can't trust you. I can't trust anybody." By the time she finished, her words were barely audible.

Cash took this in, staring at her, his heart aching. Without removing his gaze from her face, he said to Ian, "Take one of my cards from my back pocket."

"What?"

Cash twisted his head and barked, "You heard me. Get a card out of my back pocket."

Ian frowned, but did what he was told.

"Now write my cell number on it."

"Cash." His voice held a warning. "Are you sure you know what you're doing?"

"Come on, man. Write it!"

Ian pulled a pen out of the inner pocket of his coat. He shook his head, but held the card against a nearby door and began to scribble.

"You are in a world of hurt, Harper. This is too much for you to handle alone." He turned his head, keeping an arm on her chest, and took the card from Ian. He pressed it into her hand, squeezing her fingers around it, battling her resistance. "Take it," he yelled and she complied, though her jaw became set and she jutted her chin out. He regretted that little show of temper, but his nerves were shot. "I'm taking a chance on you and letting you go. You can walk away from here, or you can let us help you. The card's for if you walk away, then change your mind. You need help. You have to take a chance on somebody. I'm asking you to take a chance on me." He slowly eased off her then stepped back completely.

Harper's eyes flew to Ian. He didn't move a muscle. She looked back at Cash and sprang away, running to the end of the hall, scrambling down the stairs, and disappearing. They watched her.

Cash rubbed his eyes. "Shit." He moved his hands to his hips. "Shit!" he said louder, making a fist and laying it on the wall where she had been, leaning on his forearm. Ian remained quiet. Cash pushed off the wall, turned and walked past him. After a moment, Ian followed.

When they got back to her place Cash turned to Ian. "Well, we're here. We might as well look around for clues or some kind of evidence." He sighed. "Let's start in the back and work our way forward."

Once in the rear bedroom, Ian walked over to the closet, snatching a flashlight off a bedside table to illuminate its contents. Cash started at the dresser inside the door.

After a moment, Ian said, "This ain't your girl's room."

Cash turned, wondering over the "your girl's" rather than "our girl's." Ian held out some long pants.

"Five-Foot-Two would swim in this."

Her name's Harper.

"Toss that flashlight." Cash caught it and turned back to the drawer. He was rifling through some intimate apparel, mentally apologizing to Harper as he did so, in case it was hers, when his fingers touched something that wasn't silky. With the added illumination, he could see it was one of those strips of pictures from a photo booth. He felt around some more and came up with a pack of matches with a bar's name on it, and a slip of paper that turned out to be a marker for forty grand. He whistled.

"What?"

"The vic was in for forty grand."

Ian crossed to look at it. "If she was behind on payments, or refusing to pay, that could be the motive right there."

Inspecting it more closely, Cash realized it was actually made out to Jared Inglebrook. He flipped it over and Kitty's signature was on the back.

"Why would Harper's best friend take on her boyfriend's debt?" he wondered aloud.

Ian shrugged and pointed to the picture. "That her?"

Cash held up the picture. In it a couple were making

out. He recognized the girl as Kitty. He checked the back, but it was blank. The matchbook cover was emblazoned with The Mustard Seed, which was appropriately named because it was the seediest dive in all of Victory.

"Why would she go to that dump?"

"Good question. Better question is, how come this stuff isn't in the evidence room? You'd think Beason, or his men, would catch this."

After a thorough search of the bedroom, they did a quick look around in the living room, kitchen, and what had to be Harper's bedroom.

Knowing he was stupid for doing so, Cash couldn't help but search for any sign of Harper in the hallway and courtyard when they left the apartment. "I say we check out the bar. I could use a drink."

"I'm game. Hey, you know this isn't our case, right?"

Cash grinned. "We'll tell Beason everything we found out afterward."

"Sounds good to me."

Once downstairs, when they moved out of the shadow of the building, Cash froze so quickly Ian bumped into him. On the middle of the sidewalk in front of him, bathed in sunlight, his card sat, as if to condemn him.

He sighed, dropping his head back and proclaiming to the heavens. "I really messed that up."

Ian put a hand on his shoulder. "You did what you had to do. You took a chance." He left Cash, heading to the car.

Cash stared at the card for a moment, his hands on his hips. His jaw tightened. "Damn," he said quietly. He stepped over the card and followed Ian.

CHAPTER NINE

Cash munched on peanuts, a lukewarm beer sitting in front of him at the bar. It was not his favorite brand, but the only kind they served in bottles. And he was shocked to find they didn't carry anything on tap. What kind of bar doesn't serve draft beer?

He and Ian eyed the middle-aged bartender, waiting for a time when she wasn't as busy to ask her about Kitty Carmichael. Cash couldn't help but think they missed their opportunity when they first sat and his neighbor knocked his Budweiser can over, flooding the bar and getting some on Cash's jeans. She mopped up the mess, but seemed irritated at the time.

For a while, he and Ian made small talk, staying clear of discussing the case. They hadn't gone out together in a while. Ian's wife was expecting again, and he stuck pretty close to home. But after a bit, Cash became quieter, and Ian immersed himself in a Yankees/Red Sox game on the boxy, small screen TV that actually had rabbit ear antennas. He felt like he took a step back in time, and a step down the evolutionary scale.

Cash stared into his beer, but he wasn't seeing it. What he was seeing was Harper's frightened face, and the evidence of the abuse she suffered written on it and on her neck. Men who took advantage of their size to intimidate and hurt women made him sick. And the thought of any man even touching Harper made his blood boil.

Why is that?

What turned her from a pretty face into someone real? Someone he felt responsible for. He kept coming back to her serious answer to a lighthearted question.

A mistake.

If you asked him, Jared was the one who made the mistake in throwing away someone who seemed like a wonderful woman. Then again, the guy was low enough to steal her college money. Cash squeezed a peanut maybe a tiny bit too hard and a piece of the shell hit Ian's neck.

Ian turned.

"Sorry."

The guy the bartender was flirting with left, and she made her way to them. "Someone need another drink?"

"Yes," the both responded immediately.

She laughed. "Well, it sounds like I need to hurry and get you boys some beers." She walked away and Cash's gaze followed her blond hair. He dated mostly blondes, with a smattering of brunettes. And while Harper was a knockout as a blonde, he still preferred the red. The bartender returned with two more semi-cold bottles.

"You a Yankees fan?"

Ian grabbed some peanuts. "More of a Patriot's fan, but when it's the off season…."

"I hear you." She turned to go.

Cash quickly called her back. "Cynthia?"

"Well, yes, sugar? How did you know my name?"

I read that honkin' big rhinestone necklace that's dangling, not so subtly, between your breasts.

He smiled. "Your necklace."

"Oh, yeah." Her hand fluttered to her necklace. "So, what can I do for you?"

At the last second, he decided on a different tack. "Would you happen to know a Jared Ingelbrook?"

"No. That doesn't ring a bell."

The other bartender, who came to get the remote and change the volume on the TV, leaned over. "He means Kitty's Jared."

"Oh! Yes. Jared and Kitty are regulars."

Cash tried to hide his surprise. "Kitty? I don't think he's mentioned her. Is she a sister...?"

Both bartenders sputtered and laughed. "If she is, I think there's a coupla laws they're breaking." They high-fived each other, still cutting up.

Cash faked confusion. "What do you mean?"

The second bartender put a fist to her mouth and seemed to hold her breath waiting for the answer.

"Well, honey, you see that booth over thar?"

Cash turned.

"Well, that's Kitty and Jared's booth and we have to hose it off real good when they've been in here." Again, they busted up.

"Ahh." He forced a laugh.

Ian laughed, too, nodding his head and raising his eyebrows.

Cash slid the photo booth picture toward the pair. "This them?"

"Yup. But I haven't seen them in a coupla days, which is unusual. They're in here almost every night."

"Have they been together long, or was this kind of a recent thing?"

"Four or five years. Why are you asking? Jared owe you money? Cause I can tell you he ain't got any."

"No. It's not that. I'm adopted and trying to trace my family tree. I think we might be cousins." Cash pulled out a pen and wrote on a cocktail napkin. "Could you give him my number if you see him? I'd love to connect."

"Why sure, hon."

"Thanks."

The other bartender put her arm around Cynthia and they walked away with their heads together, tittering.

"*What* a shithead." Ian summarized.

"Yeah." He was about to say more but Ian's phone lit up and vibrate-walked into his beer bottle.

Ian snatched it up. Before he even looked at the screen, he said, "I told you. I told you she'd call."

He looked at it and smirked, turning the screen so Cash could read it. Christine, his wife, was on the line. He clicked in. Cash grinned and watched the show.

"Hey, babe. What's up?" He rolled his eyes, then he turned away slightly, his face more serious. "Did you tell her it isn't appropriate to paint her brother blue? ...on the carpet. The NEW carpet? Oh, man! Don't cry, hon. Come on. In fourteen years they'll be out of the house." He held the phone away from his ear, glanced at Cash, and hopped off his stool, taking a few steps and turning his back. "It's not your fault. You are not a bad mom. Chrissy, it's okay. Even if it doesn't come out, we can get new carpet. Eventually."

Cash drained his beer, picked up Ian's jacket, and began to walk over to him. The beer bottle in front of Ian's seat caught Cash's eye. Seemed a shame to waste good beer. He took a step back, plucked Ian's bottle off the bar and tilted it to his mouth, finishing it as well. With a satisfied smile, he set the bottle back down and grabbed his partner's sleeve on his way to the door.

"She said what? Why that little shit." Ian chuckled as Cash opened the door for him. "I'm not laughing." He cracked up. "What? I'm not laughing. Okay, Cash said something funny. No. No-o-o. *You're* the one whose laughing."

They reached the Mustang. Cash opened the passenger side door, steered Ian around it, placed his hand on top of his head, and pushed him inside. He rolled his eyes with a half-smile and got behind the wheel to take Ian home.

***

Cash flopped on his back, shifting to keep from falling off the edge of the couch. He brought his arm up, the back of his hand falling limply onto his forehead, and stared at his living room ceiling, although he couldn't see much in the dark.

Where is she sleeping right now?

His feet began to act like metronomes set to rocket speed.

Where did she sleep last night?

He huffed, turning his head to the side. Maybe he should have done something different. Maybe he should have tackled her ass and hauled her into the station over his shoulder. The thought was somehow arousing.

But she wasn't a suspect. She was a witness. That was the difference. He knew how to handle a suspect. She…. She he obviously didn't know how to handle. And if *they* found her….

He felt around on the coffee table, knocking his phone off, but snagging it in midair. He hit the home button to light the screen. Two-seventeen. Sixteen minutes later than the last time he checked. He would never sleep tonight. He threw his legs over the arm of the couch, almost kicking his empty bottles off the table and onto the floor. The house was too quiet. It didn't normally bother him, but tonight was different for some reason.

He stood, rubbing a hand across his chest and yawning. He had switched to pajama pants, but never bothered to put on the T-shirt he'd gotten out. He wasn't even sure where he put it. Stretching, he shuffled to the kitchen and opened the fridge, which abutted the archway between the two rooms, and stared inside for a couple of seconds. Moving the ketchup, he spotted the last of the six-pack he purchased after dropping Ian at his house. He twisted the cap off, laid it on the counter, took a swig from the bottle, and turned around. Movement across the room pulled his attention and he spit out his beer when he focused on an intruder.

"Holy shit!"

Her head came off the table and she flew back in the

chair. Without hesitating, she sprang for the door.

"Harper. Harper. Wait." He slid over and blocked her way. "Wait, please."

She stared at him for a heartbeat, about a foot away. She rubbed her arms and turned her back to him.

He searched for something to say. "What are you doing here?"

"I…I don't know. Maybe this wasn't a good idea." She spun, took several large strides, and tried to slip past him.

He put his hand on her sleeve, below her shoulder. "Don't leave," he said softly. "I'm glad you came." He stroked her arm, wanting to gather her in an embrace, but knowing it wasn't appropriate. She was silent, and he didn't know where he should go with the conversation. He'd been thinking about her almost non-stop, but in reality, they'd shared less than a half hour of conversation. And the one thing he needed to talk to her about, her friend's murder, was probably best left on the back burner for now.

He fell back on something he knew. Something he was taught. Manners. "Are you hungry?"

At first, she appeared to be thrown by the question, staring up at him with wide eyes. "I…." She dropped her head, hesitating. "Actually, I'm starved."

She seemed embarrassed by the admission. What did she have to be embarrassed about? He sprang into action, pulling a seat out at his kitchen table. It was round with a laminate top, a seventies throwback. Everything in the house was pretty much just as it was the night he and his parents had gone out to celebrate his birthday. The night they died.

"Please, have a seat. Let me go grab a shirt real quick." He rushed to his bedroom, found his T on top of the dresser, and wrestled it on as he walked back.

He gave her a smile when he entered. "Okay. Let's see what we've got here." He jerked open the refrigerator. "I think I have some sandwich stuff." He shifted things around, hunting for lunchmeat. "Do you like ham?"

"Um-hum."

He gathered the meat, found one last piece of cheese, and dug out some condiments, which he set on the table. Turning back to the counter, he fixed the sandwich in the only light, which came from the fixture above the sink. As he worked, he lifted his gaze to scan the back yard. Had anyone followed her? He snagged a Corel dish from the cabinet, slapped his creation on it, and placed it in front of her. Then he subtly moved over to lock the door, again peering out into the night, but seeing no movement.

I should have cut that sand—

When he turned, she was hunched over her plate and had practically wolfed down the whole sandwich. She was shoving what was left into her mouth but stopped, moving her head a little and catching him staring at her. She sat straighter, swiping a hand across her mouth.

He shook himself. "Uhh…want another sandwich? I don't think I have any more cheese, though." He crossed to double check the fridge. "Or…oh. There's an apple?"

"An apple would be good," she murmured.

He kept sifting through the contents of his fridge. "And half a bag of those baby carrots." He turned and held them up. "They're fresh. I just got them, like, a couple of days ago."

She lifted her head and smiled a little. "That would be great."

His shoulders relaxed some and he quickly rinsed the apple in the sink and brought his findings over to the table. He pulled up the seat next to her, but popped out of it seconds after he sat.

"I need to get you something to drink." It had been too long since he'd had a woman in his house. His married sister didn't count. He ate pretty simply, and wasn't used to feeding others. He got a glass and again opened the fridge. "I've got…beer," *lots of beer*, "and milk…" He withdrew the milk, unscrewed the cap and smelled it. A rank odor permeated his nostrils and he gagged. "Nope. Scratch that.

No milk." He quickly resealed it and threw it in the trash.

"Water's fine." Her smile was bigger. She was laughing at him. So what? At least she was more animated.

"That I have." He filled the glass with tap water, dug some ice out of the freezer bin, plopped them in, and brought it to her, returning to his seat.

She was chomping on the apple, but finished her bite. "This is very good. Thank you."

He shrugged. "Sure." He folded his hands on the table as she dug into the bag of carrots. "How did you find me?"

She offered him the bag, but he shook his head. "I lost your card when I ran away from you. But, believe it or not, you're the only Cash on the police force."

His lips turned up. "Yeah. Unbelievable, right?"

She raised her eyebrows. "Yes. Shocking." She took a drink, then continued. "I walked to the library and used their computer. I got your last name from the VPD website, your address from Anywho, and directions from Mapquest."

He nodded. The library. That had to be a good nine or ten miles from his house. "Then you took a cab?"

"No. I walked." When he stared, she elaborated. "I left my purse, phone, car keys…basically everything, at the casino. All I had on me was my tip money, and I used the last of that to take a taxi to my place." She frowned. "I knew they might be there, but I had to take a chance. I needed a credit card I had on my dresser. But I saw you, and…well, you know the rest."

To cover the distance from the library to his place…she must have walked for the past three hours or so. "You must be exhausted." He rose. "Let me show you to the guest room. You can get a good night's sleep and in the morning we can go down to the station."

Her chair scraped across the linoleum as she jumped to her feet. "I'm not going there. I'm not going anywhere near that station."

This caught him off guard. "What? You have to. We'll need to—"

She made a move toward the door and he stepped into her path. Her gaze flew around and he knew she was measuring her options.

"Harper. Talk to me. What's wrong?"

She looked like a cat about to spring, every nerve hunched and vibrating, but his question seemed to distract her. She turned her head, searching his face.

"They were there."

"Who?"

"The men. The men who…shot Kitty. Two of them."

"You saw them?"

She swallowed, nodding rapidly. Her eyes were hollow.

"Hanging around outside?"

"No. They were inside. Sitting—"

"Inside the station?"

"Yes. I'm not going back."

His head spun and his mouth went dry. "Can we…" He lost his train of thought. They were ballsy enough to go inside his station? "What were they doing when you saw them?"

Even in the dim light, he could see the flush coloring her cheeks, and the way her jaw tensed. "Laughing. Joking. Right after they killed her. They were sitting at their desks acting like—"

"Wait. You saw them sitting at somebody's desk?"

"No, Cash. They were sitting behind *their* desks. Policemen. Wearing regular clothes, but guns and badges at their waist."

He grabbed the top of one of the chairs. *Detectives? Were they homicide, narcotics, his own vice squad…?*

"Did you see the name plates on their desks?"

She shook her head. "No. I'm sorry. I—"

"Where? Where were their desks?"

She took half a step back. "I…" Her brows knit together. She passed a hand over the bandage on her forehead. "I don't know. I can't remember. I sort of…freaked

94

out. I spun around and tried to get out before they saw me. That place is like a maze and I got all turned around. My head was still bleeding…. I—"

"When did you go there?"

"Right after." Her forehead scrunched as she remembered. "I left the casino. I knew I needed to get help for Kitty, and tell the police what I saw. I wanted them to catch the men who did that to her."

"And when you went to the station, you saw them."

"Yes. Then, like I said, I panicked. I had to get out. I didn't know who was working with them, or who was legit, or if any of them were. I finally found a door out, but it wasn't the one I came in. I stumbled upon a pay phone a couple of blocks away and called 9-1-1. They said they'd send an ambulance for Kitty, but..." She went still. Her lip quivered for a second, then her face crumpled. She brought her hands up to cover it. "Oh, my God."

She sobbed and he stepped up to take her in his arms. She kept repeating the same things. "They killed her. They just shot her. I couldn't do anything." Then she was no longer able to talk. She wept so hard he thought she would shake apart. He didn't know what to say. There was nothing to say. He simply held her, whispered some useless words meant to comfort, smoothed his hand over her hair, and occasionally kissed the top of her head. At points, her crying changed into gut-wrenching, almost inhuman noises. Her whimpering made his heart break.

He remembered coming home for the first time after his parents' deaths and crying like that while lying in his bed, recalling every special moment with them and pre-living every occasion to come when they would not be there. And the horror of what she'd seen, he knew, too. The blood. The face of someone you loved and cared for forever stilled in death. It was almost unbearable.

After she quieted some, he helped her to the floor. He sat with his back against the cabinets, feet stretched out in front of him. She curled into him, under his arm, resting her head on his chest. His hand traveled up and down the soft skin of her arm in a rhythmic way and they both almost drifted off to sleep, but stirred at the same time. She pulled away, putting a hand on the floor to straighten her body, taking with her the warmth she'd provided him.

"I'm sorry. I'm not usually like that. I'm just so…tired." She hung her head, her opposite arm coming across her stomach, her hand clasping the elbow of her straight arm. "I don't have the strength to hold it all together right now." She fought to get the last out.

He reached across his body to put a hand under her chin and lift her head. "You don't need to apologize. I understand." He suddenly wanted to tell her about his parents, but knew it wasn't the time. It was something he rarely talked about. In fact, he'd only spoken to his sister, Dr. Hayashi, and Ian about it. His strong desire to share it with her surprised him.

Her gaze traveled between his eyes. "I shouldn't have come here." She scrambled to her feet and he hurried to rise with her.

"Wait. Why? Did I do something?"

"No." She glanced away and back, a new fire in her eyes. "Cash, people get hurt when I'm around."

"You mean the doctor?" he rushed on without waiting for her answer. "Because he's fine."

"What?"

"I called earlier, and he's stable. He lost a lot of blood. But apparently the cut wasn't deep enough to do any permanent damage."

The tension melted off her face. "That's fantastic." She clapped her hands together, then tilted her head and studied him. "You're not just saying that, are you?"

He laughed. "No. And, besides, you don't have to worry about me. I'm a professional. I'm trained to handle situations like this."

"That may be, but risks are still involved."

"Risks I was willing to take when I put my badge on."

"And that's admirable, Cash. It is. But I'm not sure I'm willing to risk your life—"

He smiled. "Has anyone ever told you you're stubborn?"

She stared at him, but her lips twitched. "Yes. I think my dad has every day of my life. But I got it from him, so he really can't say anything."

"Ahh. Well, we can argue about this in the morning." He took her hand. "Let me show you to the guest room."

She followed. "Do you really want to argue about it in the morning?"

He looked at her as they traipsed down the hall. "I'd really rather you take my word on it."

She acted like she was thinking about it. "Nah. We'll argue about it in the morning."

"So," he said as they reached the bedroom door. "I have that to look forward to." He opened the door. For the first time, he wished he'd done some improvements to the house. "It's not much, but—"

"It sure beats a dumpster." She moved around him and ran her hand over the quilt his mom made. Then she touched one of the rails of the big brass bed. "Thank you. I'll sleep like a princess here."

"Good. The bathroom is over there." He pointed to the corner of the room. "I'm pretty sure clean towels are in the cabinet. And I'm down the hall to your left if you need anything else."

"I'm sure I'll be good." She took a step forward, her face turning more serious. "I don't know how I'll ever be able to thank you, Cash."

He fought the lump in his throat and tried to lighten the situation. "I should thank you. I was thinking earlier this house was way too quiet. It'll be nice having you here."

He left before she could say anything else and went to double check all of the doors and windows. He wasn't taking any chances. Passing her bedroom on the way back to his, he noticed her door was open a crack, and the lights were off.

He couldn't resist peeking in as he passed. The light from the hall shined in, illuminating her. She was curled in a ball on her side facing him, but staring blankly at the wall, her hands together, under her face. She hadn't even bothered to get under the covers. The look on her face was the same shell-shocked expression he saw on the faces of many of the victims of violent crimes. His heart went out to her. Would she ever feel safe again?

CHAPTER TEN

Cash woke with a start. Someone was banging on the door. Sunlight streamed into his room. Bright sunlight. Eight o'clock sunlight.

Shit. Ian.

He flew out of bed. He didn't bother to hunt down his shirt. He'd gotten hot in the middle of the night and thrown it off somewhere. He rushed down the hall and skittered to a stop as he turned toward the front door. He could see Ian's shadow on the curtains as he raised his fist to knock again.

Shit. If he wakes her, I'll kick his ass.

Cash messed with the locks and whipped the door open. Ian stood with his hand still raised.

"What the hell? Did you oversleep?"

"Shh!" Cash yanked his partner into the house and clamped a hand over his mouth. "Keep it down."

A big grin cut Ian's face. He whispered, "What? Did you get lucky last night?"

Cash didn't dignify that with an answer. He took Ian's arm and dragged him down the hall to the guest room door.

"Ouch. Geez, man. What's up with—"

Cash nudged the door open wider. Harper's pajama pants lay on the floor, and she had gotten under the covers at some point. She was in a similar position, though, with her hands curled near her face.

"You *did* get lucky."

Cash smacked him on the back of the head.

"Ouch. What?"

"It's Harper, you idiot."

His mouth fell open and he looked again. "Wow. She actually trusted you."

"Yes, she actually trusted me," he hissed. Cash pushed him toward the living room.

When they came to a stop, Ian turned to look at him again. "You don't have a shirt on. Did you and she...you know?"

He wanted to slap the grin off Ian's face, but he settled on hitting him on the shoulder. "No, she and I didn't...you know! She's fragile. Do you think I'd take advantage of a girl in that condition?"

"Well." Ian wiggled his eyebrows. "Did you?"

He rolled his eyes. Turning his back, he stomped into the kitchen and straight over to the coffee pot. He looked at the clock on the stove. The coffee had been ready for an hour. He got a cup, and despite being annoyed with Ian, got one for him, too. He poured, handed Ian his cup, and they both leaned against his counter and drank. They carpooled to work together every morning. Cash drove the Mustang so Ian's family car wouldn't have the extra miles on it, and he left the sedan in front of Cash's place.

"So we're waiting until she wakes on her own then heading to the station together? Or are you waking her at some point?"

Cash turned to pour some more coffee and figure out how to answer Ian's questions.

"Well..."

"We're taking her to the station, right, Cash?" Ian stared at him. "Because, that is what we should do. Take her to the station."

"She doesn't want to go—"

"Oh, no. Here we go." Ian slammed his cup on the

counter.

"Sh-sh-sh. Will you shut up already?" He walked over and stuck his head in the hall, looking toward the bedrooms and listening for any movement. Not hearing any, he came back over. "There's a perfectly good reason why we can't—"

"Perfectly good reason," he scoffed. "I'll tell you what your 'perfectly good reason' is. You want to get it on with—"

Cash stepped up, really pissed now. "Don't you talk like that. Don't say that again."

Ian put his hands up. "Whoa. Back down, bro."

Cash stared at him for a tense moment, then eased up a fraction. "Let's get something straight here. She," he stabbed his finger in the air in the direction of the bedrooms, "has been through hell and back, and she doesn't need your bullshit."

"No bullshit intended. Cool it." He picked his cup up again and held it below his mouth before taking another sip. "Gee. Somebody's grouchy."

Cash stood with his arms folded considering his actions. He decided he might have gotten a bit out of hand. He picked up his cup and stared out the window as he drank. "Sorry. I haven't slept much lately."

"Okay." He seemed to be choosing his words carefully now. "So what's the good reason we're not going to the station?"

Cash looked at his partner. "Because we've got bad cops down there, and until I know what's going on, I'm not taking her to the station."

Ian's cup went down on the counter again. "Bad cops? And you know this because…?"

"Because Harper saw them when she went to report seeing Kitty being shot. The guys who shot her are detectives."

Ian stared. He opened his mouth to say something, closed it, then turned a little circle in the kitchen with his hands on his hips. "So you're taking the word of a girl you met like, two days ago, over the word of your brothers in blue who you've known for most of your professional career."

"I haven't known all of them that long. And I'm not taking her word for it. I'm investigating. But until I know for sure what's going on, I'm not risking her life by bringing her in."

"What about taking her to the Buffalo PD, or, better yet, some small town where she can hold up?"

"I thought about that. If we miss work, they'll know she's with us. They'd put out a APB on us…. I don't know. I think this is the best place for her to be right now, until we figure a few things out."

"Okay. But let's say they are watching the house. Won't my being here look a tad suspicious?"

"Not with your and Chrissy's marital problems."

"Wait. We have marital problems?"

"Well, that's what I'm telling the captain. And you're taking a few days off to sort things out."

"Okay, but I leave here every night."

"You and Chrissy want everything to look normal for the kids."

"You know we're really not having marital problems, right?"

"Yeah."

"Good. 'Cause you're starting to sound like you believe your own stories." Ian chewed on this for several seconds. "So what now?"

"I thought I'd go in and start trying to find this Jared. He seems to be mucked up in the middle of this somehow."

"And I get to babysit the redhead."

"Blonde," Cash corrected.

"Blonde. Well, I can think of worse things." He smiled like a predator.

"Don't be getting any ideas. You're married, and she's off the list."

Ian picked up his coffee. "You're a real party pooper, you know that, Cash?"

"Yes." He glanced at the stove again. "And this party pooper needs to get going." He set his cup in the sink and turned to go, but after a few seconds stuck his head back in the doorway. "And when I get to the station, I'm sending you mug shots for Harper to look at, so you're not totally off the hook work-wise today."

He grinned and left, but heard Ian mutter, "Swell."

As he passed Harper's door, she reached out and grabbed him, tugging him into the room. She hadn't put her pajama pants on yet, and all the skin of those legs....

Have mercy.

"Cash. Who is that?" she whispered hoarsely. He could see she was trembling now. Shit. He hadn't thought about how hearing a male voice might make her feel.

He grasped her upper arms. "It's just Ian, my partner. Remember? He was with me yesterday at your place. He's cool."

"Oh." She didn't elaborate, simply shifted her weight from side to side, and brought her hand to her mouth, rubbing it over her lips.

"Hey. Are you okay? You're shaking."

"Oh. Yeah. I'm...uh. I'm fine. Just cold." She looked at her bare legs and a faint blush rose to her cheeks. "Okay, then." She herded him to the door. "I'll get dressed."

He leaned back in. "Help yourself to any of the clothes in the dresser, and anything in the bathroom."

"Okay. Thanks." She closed the door on him.

Cash smiled and hurried to jump in the shower.

When he came out, she was in the kitchen with Ian, her hair wet, a cup of coffee raised to her lips. He sensed he was interrupting an awkward conversation.

She sprang to her feet, putting the cup down at the same time. "Oh. Hi."

"Hi." A smile slid across his face. She was wearing some of his sister's clothes, but they didn't look "sisterly" on her. Was it wrong to be a wee bit turned on by that? Maybe he chose the wrong person to go into work.

No. It has to be me. I'll see her tonight, he added, to reassure himself.

She scratched her head, tilting it toward the hall. "Can I just…" She pushed him toward the door. "I'll be back in a minute," she said, smiling at Ian. But when she had him in the hall alone, her demeanor changed. "Cash," she whispered urgently. "He said you were going in to the station."

"Yes. If we both don't show it'll—"

"Couldn't he go?" She glanced over her shoulder. Ian was looking out the window. "Cash, I…." She put a hand on his arm, rocking onto the balls of her feet, then removed it bringing her hands together to fold them. "It's just I…." She threw a look back again, then leaned in, returning her hand to his arm, and holding on like she'd never let go. "I feel safer when you're here."

Warmth flooded through him. "Well, that's very flattering, but—"

"Please, Cash. I—" She looked over and Ian waved at her with a smile. She waved awkwardly, but guided Cash farther down the hall. "Maybe I could go and stay in your car."

"All day?"

She shrugged. "I've been in worse positions."

"Harper." He bent to establish better eye contact with her. "I *swear* to you. I know he's a little…" Cash peered into the kitchen. Ian was messing around in his sugar bowl. "…goofy. But he is the best cop I've ever worked with, hands down."

"Well…." She twisted to check Ian out again. Her hands were back at her mouth and she was chewing on her nails. "What time will you be back?"

"Six or seven. Eight at the latest."

"*Eight!*" She moaned. "Okay. But hurry home if you can."

He gave her a smile and patted her arms. "I will. I

promise." He raised his voice. "I'm heading out now. Lock this door behind me."

"Got it." Ian already sounded bored.

"I'll be home as soon as I can," he repeated to Harper.

He felt wistful as he drove away, glancing back and half-hoping to catch Harper at the big bay window in the living room. But he knew that wouldn't be smart.

***

It was almost lunchtime and Cash was no closer to finding Jared Inglebrook than he had been when he arrived at work. He hoped Ian and Harper were having better luck with the mug shots he'd sent to his laptop. They'd gotten nowhere with identifying the dirty cops through online photos. Which could mean only one thing. They worked undercover. The chief didn't exactly advertise those guys on the police roster. Cash toyed with the idea of asking his captain for clearance to look at personnel files, but he was afraid this would draw questions. He'd spent much of the morning trying to subtly take pictures of his coworkers with his phone. When he'd sent the images to her via text, none of them were the men she'd seen. It was a big station, and too much roaming around to take shots would be suspicious.

"Hey, Cash."

Mike Beason approached, waving at another detective before pulling up a chair and straddling it, crossing his arms on top of the back. "I thought I'd come and compare notes and see if you'd come up with anything." He nodded across at Ian's empty desk. "Where's Ian?"

"He took a personal day." Until he had them checked out, everyone was a suspect, even his captain. Beason was no exception.

He glanced at the photo strip on his desk. "Who's that?"

Cash picked it up and handed it to him. "Name's Jared Inglebrook. He's the witness's boyfriend."

Beason slid out his notebook, but before he opened it he did a double take. "Isn't that the victim?"

"Yep."

His eyebrows shot up and he studied the picture closer. "I don't get it. How's a guy like that wind up with two beautiful girls like—hey, wait a minute. Didn't you tell me the vic and the witness were best friends."

"Yep," Cash repeated, leaning back and lacing his fingers on top of his head.

"What a schmuck."

"Agreed. And I can't find anything on him. Apparently he doesn't have a job, and hasn't had one in six years."

"Sponging off women?"

Cash nodded. "That would be my guess."

Beason looked back at the picture. "Isn't he older than both Kitty Carmichael and that Harper?"

Cash nodded, straightening and taking the picture back. He examined it again himself before setting it down. "Quite a bit."

"Where'd you find that, by the way?"

"Carmichael's apartment. Where I didn't see your men posted."

Beason grinned. "They saw you."

He blinked. "You, serious?"

"Yeah. Well, you didn't expect them to be sitting out in the open, did you? That would alert the witness and anyone after her."

"No. But I thought I'd spot them."

"Maybe you're not as good as you think you are."

"Maybe. But highly doubtful. Why didn't they find this?" He tapped on the picture.

Beason frowned. "Good question. Where did you find it?"

"In Kitty Carmichael's dresser."

He shook his head. "They're rookies, but they should have found this. I'll be having a talk with them. Find anything else?"

Cash pushed the marker his way and Beason picked it up. He whistled. "Man. Forty grand. I'd call that motive for murder." He flipped it over. "Miss Kitty was taking on this Jared guy's debt. When were you going to tell me about this?"

"Shoulda brought it to you this morning. Sorry."

He rose. "Nah. No problem. You've done good work here, Delmanaco. Ever think of joining Homicide?"

"That's where I wanted to be when I came out of the academy, but there weren't any openings at the time."

"I'll keep my eyes peeled for you. We could use a detective of your caliber over there."

"Thanks."

Beason turned to go.

"Hey, Mike. Got any info for me?"

He rapped on Cash's desk. "I'm sorry to say no. You've turned up way more than any of the rest of us have. Must be motivated, huh?"

Cash didn't bite. "Just working the case."

"Uh-huh. See ya."

Cash shook his head and refocused on his computer screen.

There had to be a clue to this guy's whereabouts somewhere.

In his peripheral vision, he saw Hank Bedford, another vice detective, heading in his direction. He quickly pushed a button to switch screens.

"Why does Beason have his business all up in here?"

Cash smiled at his wording. "We're working a case together. You going to lunch?"

"Yeah. I saw Ian is out and thought I'd ask you if you'd want to join me."

"Nah. I'm not hungry," he lied, and his stomach protested quietly, reminding him that he'd skipped breakfast.

"You sure? I could bring you back something."

"That'd be great. In case I get hungry later." He gave

Hank his order and he left. The squad room was empty. Great time to call and check on Ian.

CHAPTER ELEVEN

It was two-thirty, and Harper was cross-eyed and tuning out. Who knew so many suspicious characters existed in the world? Even with narrowing the search by color of hair and texture, there were still hundreds of mug shots to go through. She only wished she knew his eye color. She was slumped over a desk in the far corner of Cash's living room, one elbow planted on the black surface, chin in her hand, the other grasping the clicker. Realizing her mouth was hanging open, she closed it, and glanced over at Ian.

He was sitting on the sofa with his feet on Cash's coffee table. A pizza box was open about two inches from his left foot. The man was a bulldozer with food. He'd eaten practically every food item in the fridge and cabinets, ordered two large pizzas and eaten all but the two pieces she'd eaten and the three left in the second box.

Make that two, she amended when she noticed he was stuffing another slice into his mouth.

"Ian," she whined. "Can't I take a break? I've been going at it for hours."

"No," he said without even bothering to look over.

"Five minutes. I've been staring at the screen so long the pictures are blurring again."

"Okay," he conceded, as if it somehow pained him to let her stretch her legs.

Harper got up and placed her hands on the small of her back, arching backward. Ian burped and she scowled at him.

"What?" He looked at her with rounded eyes. "Oh, excuse me."

She shook her head in disgust, snagged her glass, and plodded into the kitchen. She opened the freezer to get some fresh ice and spotted it, shining like the Holy Grail.

"I-an," she called in a singsong voice. "Wanna make this more fun." She swung a bottle of Jaegermeister in front of her.

He sat forward, looking more animated. "What do you have in mind?"

She held the bottle up and looked at it as if it had the answer. "Let's say…every ten mug shots I look at, we drink a shot."

His smile was huge. "Now you're talking."

***

It was well after dark, and Harper and Ian were sitting on the floor with their legs under the coffee table, backs against the couch. The pizza box still sat in front of them, but only a few pieces of crust remained. It was mainly acting as a coaster for the quickly dwindling Jägermeister and their two shot glasses. They had abandoned the mug shots long ago. Harper poured, touched her glass to his, then drained it. She wiped the back of her hand over her mouth. She was getting sloppy.

"We clinked. We drinked." Ian laughed at his joke, but Harper went on as if she didn't hear him.

"So yeah," she said loosely. "I walk in, and they're going at it on the couch we bought with the rest of my scholarship money."

"No!"

"Is your head wobbling? Or is it my vision?"

Ian put his hand on his head, messing his hair even

further. He giggled. "My head's wobbling." They both laughed and fell over, bonking their heads together.

Ian snorted. "Ouch."

"Oh. That hurt." Harper's stomach rolled, but she ignored it.

"S-s-so, what did you do?"

"What could I do? This prostitute is riding my boyfriend in the middle of my living room in broad daylight."

Ian blinked, appearing to have some difficulty focusing on her. His eyes were drooping. "Did you hit her?"

"No!"

"Oh." He seemed to think about this. "Did you hit him?"

Harper swatted Ian's shoulder, but mostly missed and hit the couch. "No. And do you know what he said to me?"

"No. Because I wasn't there."

"That's right. He said, 'Well, I didn't pay her.' Like that somehow made it better."

"What a loser. Why did you stay with him?"

"I thought I loved him."

Ian nodded. "O-ohh." He lifted his head, although this seemed to take some effort on his part. "Harper."

Several seconds passed. "Yes, Ian."

"You're…" He lifted a hand, furrowing his brow as he stared at her and slowly brought a finger up. It hit her nose, slid off, and landed on her lips, which apparently was where he intended for it to go as he smiled in triumph. "Sh-sh."

"Okay. Okay," she whispered.

He concentrated again, moving his finger jerkily around her mouth. "You're a very pretty girl."

She stared at him and got the sense something important was going on. Something she needed to pay attention to. She puckered her mouth, took hold of his finger, and bent it back toward him.

"Ouch. Ouch. Woman!"

"And you're a very married man." She released his finger and put several more inches of room between them.

Ian examined his finger. "Cash told you that, di'n't he?"

"Yep."

"Figures." He sat straighter, looking around the room, his head lolling on his shoulders. "I guess I'm sorry and all that."

"It's not me you should be saying sorry to."

"It's not?"

"No! You should apologize to your wife."

"Chrissy?" His voice rose in volume and in pitch.

She nodded. A little more strongly than she intended to. "Yes."

Ian smiled, letting his head fall back onto the couch cushion. "I love her."

"If you love her so much, why did you hit on me?"

"Well…" He seemed to lose his train of thought. Harper forgot she even asked him a question when he blurted out, holding his palms out to her. "You are very attractive."

It was as if he were blaming her. "Well, thank you, but—"

"You're welcome." He burped. He held an unsteady finger to his mouth. "Sh-sh-sh. She doesn't like that," he whispered loudly.

"I don't." Harper grabbed a piece of pizza crust and gnawed on it. "What was I saying?"

"I don't know."

She waved the pizza crust at him. "We need to sober you up. Cash is gonna be pissed."

Ian made an attempt to push to his feet. "Cash is always pissed. He needs to get laid."

"Huh. Judging from all of the women's clothing in the dresser in the guest room, I'd say that happens on a pretty regular basis." She sighed, struggling to her feet, too.

"What? Oh. That shit is his sister's."

She was about to pick the pizza box up, but stopped.

"His sister's?"

Ian grabbed a roll of paper towels they used for napkins. And spills. "Yeah. She lives out in the country and will stay here sometimes when something's going on in town. Or if she needs to get away from her husband and the kids."

She smiled. "Really?"

"Aw, yeah. He's too busy saving the world and shit. I guess the cape gets in the way when it comes to getting laid or something."

"Hmm…." Headlights swung across the curtains. She gave a little squeak. "Speak of the devil." She got on her hands and knees and picked up several pieces of crust that had escaped their attention. She shoved it at Ian. "Get rid of this!" She picked up the Jägermeister bottle as Cash was coming in and hid it behind her back. Ian froze halfway to the kitchen with the pizza box. They both smiled.

Cash slowly pulled his keys out of the door, examining the pair. "What's going on?"

"Nothing. Right, Ian?"

"Nothing. Like she said."

Cash closed the door and set his keys on the end table. "Uh-huh." He stuck his hands in his pockets. "What's behind your back?"

Ian shot a glance at Harper. "You're on your own." He ducked into the kitchen.

"Coward," she mumbled out of the side of her mouth.

Cash moved forward, and she took a step back. He lunged, catching her, and causing her to scream. He wrestled the bottle from her hand and brought it out where he could see it. Ian ran in, his concerned gaze darting to Harper. He stopped and put a hand over his heart, leaning against the side of the archway between the two rooms.

"Hmm." Cash tilted the bottle. "Is this my Jäger?"

Ian and Harper looked at each other with open mouths, but neither spoke.

Cash ambled over to the coffee table and clinked the

bottle against the shot glasses as he set it down. "So—and correct me if I'm wrong—it looks like, while I've been out working my ass off, the two of you were busy getting snockered."

"Oh, no." Harper shook her head. "We were working hard, right, Ian?"

Ian made an attempt to stand straight but swayed comically. "We were working hard." He nodded, then turned to Harper. "What were we working hard at again?"

"Looking at the mug shots."

"Oh. Yeah. That's right. We were looking at the mug shots." He faced Cash. "And doing shots."

"Sh-sh-sh. It's a secret." Harper laughed.

Ian chuckled along with her. "Oh, yeah."

Cash put his hands on his hips. "Well, I hate to tell you, friends, but the cat's out of the bag now."

"Cat? What cat?" Harper cracked up again.

"He has a cat?" Ian seemed genuinely confused, looking around for the feline. "You never told me you had a cat."

Harper sputtered and broke into laughter again.

Cash put his feet on the coffee table, spreading his arms out along the top of the couch. "Whose idea was this anyhow?"

They pointed at each other.

"It was mine?" Harper asked. Ian nodded. "Oh. It was mine." She smiled and didn't try to hide her pride.

Cash shook his head and pulled out his phone. "Okay, Ian. I'm calling you an Uber." He punched some buttons. "Chrissy's gonna kick your butt. And the next time she sees me, she's gonna kick my butt." He looked at his screen. "Two minutes away." He came over and put his arm around Ian, steering him to the door.

"I'm leaving?"

Cash grabbed his jacket off a recliner. "Yes, you are. Maybe the night air will sober you up some."

"I doubt it."

114

Cash laughed. "I doubt it, too. And you, little missie—" he swung around to point to her.

She looked about, then put a finger on her chest and mouthed "Me?"

"Yes, you. Don't think you're off the hook. I'll deal with you when I get back."

She held onto the back of a chair, swinging her hips from side to side. "Ooh!"

He snickered. "Stay. There. And don't get into any more trouble."

She plucked his uniform hat off the other end table, where she had been messing with it early in the drinking binge. She stuck it on her head and gave him a lazy salute. "Yes, sir."

He chuckled. "Oh, boy."

"Nite, Harper," Ian called. She smiled at him. He looked at his finger, then whispered loudly to Cash, "You need to watch out for that one. She plays dirty sometimes."

"Really?" Cash looked back with a puzzled expression. Ian passed through the door, and Cash paused on the threshold for a moment, gazing at her. Her heart soared. Then he stepped out, and was gone.

When he came in a few moments later, she was stretched out on the couch, still wearing his cap. He shut the door with a sigh then meandered over to her.

"You are a very naughty girl."

She curled her legs up, trying to look sexy. "Am I?"

"Yes." He bent over to pick up the bottle, which she had knocked off the table while he was out with Ian. While his back was turned, Harper made her way to her feet, balancing on a couch cushion. When he straightened, she launched herself onto his back, wrapping her arms around his neck.

He laughed, putting a hand up to try to help support her. "What the hell are you doing?"

"Ian said you have a cape. I want to see your cape. Where is it?" She held on and yanked on his shirt to look

115

down his back.

He sputtered and moved backward a few steps. In range of the couch again, she put her feet down. He spun and brought his arms under her knees, scooping her up and turning to sit on the couch with her in his lap.

"I'm not showing you my cape." His voice was a low rumble. It vibrated with amusement, and maybe something more.

He smelled wonderfully good, and having his arms around her was heaven.

Without even really thinking about it, she brought her hands up and began to unbutton her shirt. "I'll show you my cape if you show me yours."

She didn't know what made her do it. Was it the alcohol? Was it having a few moments to let go of the hurt and fear that made her giddy? Whatever was causing her to feel this way, she had an overwhelming need to open herself to him, to lay herself bare before him.

His big, soft hands came up to cover hers. "Not this way." The moment stretched out. Her earlier fuzziness seemed to disappear and she suddenly felt like she saw with such clarity.

"I like you, Cash."

He brushed the hair back from her face then trailed the backs of his fingers along her cheek. When he spoke, his words came out slowly, carefully. "Well, I like you, Harper."

She ducked her head. "You're not mad at me?"

He smiled, his eyes twinkling in the lamplight. "No. Not really. If anyone deserves a drink or two, it would be you."

She laid her head on his chest. It felt right. She rubbed her hand over his pec.

"I've had more than a drink or two."

He chuckled. "No kidding."

"Ian had more." She laughed, thinking about the drunken way he had traced her lips.

"What?"

She had lost herself in the memory for a moment. "Nothing."

"Come on. What are you thinking about?"

"Just...nothing." When he continued to stare at her with a probing gaze, she waved a hand as if to dismiss it. "Just something silly Ian did."

He continued to study her features and heat rose to her cheeks. "He hit on you, didn't he?"

She opened her mouth in surprise then quickly closed it. She scooted out of his lap. "We made such a mess." She picked crumbs out of the carpeting.

"He did."

She turned around to deny it but shrugged instead. "A little. But after that he told me about how much he loves Chrissy."

"Hmm." He didn't look too happy about it.

She looked away and spotted half of an Oreo Ian had dropped and bent to get it. She turned toward the couch and caught Cash's expression. It had changed.

She smiled, coming closer to him "What are you thinking?"

His voice was gruff. "You really want to know?"

Did she? She looked into his eyes and inched closer. "Yes."

He sat up, not breaking eye contact. "I'm thinking you look way hotter in my sister's clothes than she does."

"Ian was telling the truth." She sat next to him.

He laughed. "I doubt it, but what do you think he was telling the truth about?" His brow wrinkled.

She ran a hand along his forehead, smoothing out the wrinkles. "He told me those clothes were your sister's."

"Whose did you think they were?"

"I thought they were your conquests."

"Ha," he sputtered. "Not hardly."

She skimmed her fingers along his jawline, cupping his face softly. "He told me your cape got in the way."

His hands came around her legs, but he laughed. "Oh,

that's where the cape came from."

She peered into his eyes and saw sadness for the first time, and it struck her. Struck her so she could hardly breathe. "Why do you want to save the world?"

He hesitated. "Do you really want to know?"

She shifted to drape herself across his lap again. He took her in so readily. "Yes. I want to know all about you, Cash."

He ran a finger under her collar and she wanted to be like a cat, stretching into the palm of their owner. "I'm not sure this is the right time."

"It's something serious."

"Yes."

"I can be serious."

"Can you?" He looked toward the window and she waited silently. Hoping he would trust her with his story. He took a deep breath. "Okay." He sat straighter and his arms fell away. She slid onto the couch next to him. "On my twelfth birthday, my parents took me out to Mario's Pizzeria, on Fifth Street."

"Oh, I know that place."

"Yeah. Great pizza. It was my favorite."

The way he said *was* made her stomach drop away, and a chill crept along her arms. "What happened?"

He looked toward the coffee table, but she could tell he wasn't really seeing it. He was back on that night. Back on a night that had apparently changed him. "We were walking back to the car. This guy was hiding between the cars and he came up behind my mom and put a gun to her head."

Her chest tightened.

"He was wearing a ski mask. My dad begged him to let her go, took everything out of his pockets and put it on the hood of the car, telling him to take it. Take it all. I was on my dad's side of the car and I could see he was shaking. My dad was a Marine. He wasn't afraid of anything." He paused.

Had she wanted to say anything, she was incapable of doing so.

"Then the guy started…messing with my mom. Saying, 'Where are *your* goods, sugar? Pretty thing like you probably got some nice goods.' He…touched her, and my dad lost it. He screamed at the guy to get his hands off her. The guy turned toward us, raised the gun, and shot him. He fell to his knees. His hands squeaking along the hood of the car as he fell. My mom broke free, screaming out his name. The guy grabbed her, spun her around and hit her across the face. She fell back against the car, her head to one side, and moaned. She spit out blood, then caught my eye. This look—" His voice broke, and a single tear spilled over his lashes. "Geez. I'm sorry." He rubbed the tear away with the base of his palm.

"No, Cash." She wanted to say more, but couldn't. Tears were streaming down her face unchecked.

He leaned forward, elbows on his knees, hands folded. "Uhh…she got this real…determined look. I don't even know how to describe it. It was as if she was telling me, without saying anything, everything would be all right. She turned to face the guy, and he put the gun to her forehead and squeezed the trigger. I heard her body hit the ground. One noise. All at once." He gestured with his hand. "I was screaming out her name and crying." He rubbed a hand over his face and left it on his chin. "He walked around the front of the car and I sort of shrank down and curled in a ball, wrapping my arms around my legs. He looked at me, looked at my dad, who wasn't moving, and shot him again. In the chest. He raised the gun and pointed it at me. A single strand of smoke rose and disappeared in the parking lot lights. 'How about you, squirt? You wanna get popped,too?' I couldn't speak. He walked closer, crouched, and let his arms rest on his thighs, the gun dangling between them. He was only, maybe, a foot from me. He pressed the muzzle to my forehead. I closed my eyes. Ready for it. He told me I wasn't worth the ammo and walked away, leaving me with the bodies of my parents in an empty parking lot, at eight o'clock at night, by myself. They never caught the bastard."

Having finished his recitation, Cash hung his head, looking exhausted. Harper pressed a curled hand to her mouth, forcibly holding in the sobs that wanted to tear from her body. She began to shake violently, and it felt so odd. Like her body staged a coup. He must have felt the tremors because his head flew up.

"Oh, my God. What the hell is wrong with me?" He snatched a throw blanket off the back of the couch and wrapped it around her, drawing her body into his. She took a loud, shaky breath. "Oh, God, honey. I'm so sorry." He stretched out on the couch and curled her in so she was almost on top of him.

She wanted to speak. To tell him it was okay. To do anything she could to relieve his pain. He laid his cheek near her temple. They lay like that, and Harper fought to take in air, deep shaky breaths. She squeezed her eyes tightly and fought away the sobs. She would not fall apart on him. He whispered things to her and she thought consciously about each part of her body, trying to mentally relax them. After a bit, the shaking became weaker. He lay with his back against the arm of the couch and she curled into his armpit. The arm on the outside of the couch held her securely. The other arm flopped over his head. She stirred. Had it been twenty minutes? An hour? She tilted her head to look at him. He was staring at the ceiling, but became aware of her movement and brought his arm down, lifting his head so he could look at her.

"You okay?"

She nodded rapidly, and he laid his head back. She slowly moved her hand over to his arm and stroked him. He didn't react. She pushed up so she could look into his face. Thinking of all he'd told her, she wanted to cry again. She brought her fingertips to brush along the stubble on his cheeks. He watched her, but didn't move. She lowered herself, bringing her lips to his slowly. The kisses were gentle, tentative at first, but when he responded something flashed within her. A fierce need for more of him. She took the kisses deeper.

He brought his hands to the side of her face, forgetting, or unaware of the bruising along her left side where she had been punched. The pain was intense, but evoked a strange sweetness in it. Then it disappeared as he buried his hands in her hair. He took over. His kisses were hungry, hard, and searching. He flipped so he was above her. The power of his body turned her on. He drove his hands beneath her, under her shirt, bunching her top, traveling over skin, owning every part of her. His fingers were spread wide and possessively around her rib cage. She moaned, pushing into him, her body alive. His lips traveled lower, around her chin and down her neck. She closed her eyes, savoring the sensations he was creating.

Then it stopped.

Her lids fluttered open. His gaze was fixed on her neck. He pushed off and scrambled to his feet, his back to her, hands on his hips, head lowered. She lifted onto her elbows so she could watch him.

"I, uhh, shouldn't have done that. I'm sorry. I…uhh…." He sighed, running his hand harshly across his face. "I, umm…." He took a few steps forward and stopped. He turned to face down the hallway to the bedrooms. He threw a quick glance in her direction, then looked away. "It's late."

It can't be much past ten.

"You didn't sleep well last night. I didn't sleep well last night. Perhaps we should go to bed." He rubbed the back of his neck, then grimaced and extended his hand in front of him. "I could…walk you to your room, if you'd like."

She stared at him, breathless and confused. How was she supposed to respond to that? There didn't seem to be much of a choice, so she slowly swung around, sitting and placing her feet on the floor, hands flat on the couch.

I guess we're going to bed?

Pushing her way to standing, she looked in his direction again. He made no eye contact.

What did I do?

She hesitantly crossed to him. He gave her a tight smile and took a step back to let her pass. She headed toward her bedroom, puzzled by his actions and not knowing how to behave herself now.

She stopped at her doorway and he stood as far away from her as the hallway would allow. One hand was tucked stiffly behind his back, and he ran the other one through his hair while he waited for her to turn the knob.

"Goodnight. I hope you sleep well."

He hurried down the hall, entered his room, and closed the door. She was utterly perplexed. Embarrassed and stung by his rejection, too. She shuffled to bed and tried not to think about it.

CHAPTER TWELVE

Cash leaned against his bedroom door, both hands grasping the knob behind his back. What the hell had just happened? He moved over to the bed and lowered himself to a seated position on the edge of the mattress, scratching his head.

Let's see...I dumped a hellish story on a girl who is still in shock over her own recent horrors.... He squeezed his eyes closed, remembering the image of her curled on her side the night before, staring blankly at the wall. *Then, when she felt sorry for me and kissed me I, like, mauled her.* Flashes of the past several minutes fired through his head, along with the sensations she created. Those beautiful eyes of hers, looking on him with tenderness and concern. The feel of her soft lips, his parting tentatively in return for that first taste of her. Then the images came faster, slamming into him. Her fragrance filling him, the way her skin felt as his hands dove under her shirt, skimming along the indention of her waist, the almost unbearable want and need driving him, the blood pounding through his veins...then, as his lips brushed along her neck, the sucker punch seeing her bruises had given him.

He fell back on the mattress and slapped himself in the head. A frustrated groan left his lips, and he hoped she didn't hear him. How could he do that to her? The words he'd spoken to Ian that morning came back to taunt him.

123

"She's fragile. Do you think I'd take advantage of a girl in that condition?"

Apparently, yes. You would.

He got up and trudge to his small bathroom. He snapped on his light and stared at his reflection in the medicine cabinet mirror.

You're no better than that damned Jared.

He shook his head in disgust, brushed his teeth, undressed, and got under the covers. Arms crossed under his head on the pillows, he lay with eyes wide open. Why did he tell her about his parents? He'd kept that from everybody. Was it because he felt with what she'd gone through with Kitty, she would understand it?

Yes. Of course, that's it. In other words, you were being a selfish prick.

He flipped onto his side, leaving a hand under his head and staring at the light seeping in under the door. He'd forgotten to turn the hall light out. He briefly considered getting up to switch it off. Very briefly. Something was still buzzing around at the periphery of his brain like an annoying gnat. He had other women in his life. He riffled through his mental Rolodex. All nice women. Intelligent. ...the physical aspect was always satisfying. But he'd never told one of them about that night, and he'd told her. A girl he'd known for a couple of days. Why? It wasn't only because of their common traumatic experiences. What then?

He had a Superman complex. She'd said it herself. Always needing to save someone. And if anyone needed saving right now, it was Harper. But how, exactly, did that fit into the puzzle? He needed to save her...but telling her about a night when he was twelve wouldn't do anything to help that.

Okay. This whole sleep thing is not happening.

Without putting any thought into it, he did what he always did when he couldn't sleep. Tried to work out some of the stress so he could relax and drift off. He dug out a pair of old gray sweats and put them on. He'd start with push-ups.

He got into plank position, dropped, and pushed himself away from the floor. Over and over. But being in that position reminded him of how he hovered over Harper and how she pressed into him, and….

Damn. This isn't going well. Sit ups.

He switched to lying on his back and doing crunches. He got ten in, concentrating on his form. But on the eleventh, as he lowered himself back, he saw her rising above him like she did, looking at him with such sweet compassion, it soothed an ache inside of him.

He huffed and added twists to his crunches as he rose. Left side. Right side. But engaging his abs made him think of when he'd lifted her, before things got carried away, and brought her to the couch. She was wearing his hat and it looked damned cute on her.

Side planks. Surely, side planks will work.

But he'd wrapped her in the blanket and hugged her close to his side. It didn't matter what stance he was in; he couldn't get her out of his head. He liked everything about her. The way, when her hair hung over her shoulder, it had soft curls at the ends. The way she was with Ian when he walked in. Funny, yes. Hysterical. But he could also tell they'd bonded. And there's nothing better than introducing a new friend to an old friend and having them hit it off. The way she was loyal to Ian even when the s.o.b. hit on her, which he definitely would be answering for in the morning. Cash sat on his rear, knees up, forearms resting on them as he thought about all this. The sexy way she said, "I'll show you my cape if you show me yours."

Cash spied the jump rope. Okay. No way was jumping rope reminding him of her by any stretch. He got up and reached under a chair for the wooden handles that peeked out and got to work. He jumped and jumped. Then pushed himself further and faster.

A rap on the door startled him.

"Cash?"

It's her. Of course it is, you idiot. Who else would it

be?

"Uhh…yes?"

Shit. I'm all sweaty.

He spotted the towel from his morning shower still lying in a heap on the floor and swooped it up on his way to the door, running it across his chest.

"I was just—"

He opened the door. Her eyes went wide, and she looked away.

"Oh, umm…I was wondering what was going on. Because I heard a weird sound. Several of them, actually."

He still held the jump rope in a hand. "I was working out. Sorry to wake you."

Her gaze, which was looking anywhere but at him, now rested on his face, her brow furrowed. "Do you always work out at one-thirty in the morning?"

"No. It's not that late." He looked over at his alarm clock. One-forty-two. "Oh, wow. I guess it is that late. I lost track of time."

"You must be in great shape to work out and lose track of time. I've never worked out and lost track of time. Yea. I mean of course you are in great shape. Anybody could see you are in great shape. Not that I was staring or anything…I, yea, I heard those noises and…I wanted to see if you were okay. Which you are. Better than okay actually, but…anyway. I'm gonna head back on over there," she gestured to her room, "and, you know, try to get back to sleep. So…sleep well." She turned and tried to scurry away but he caught her hand.

"Harper." When she turned back, he dropped her hand. "I want to apologize for…my strange behavior earlier. I don't know why I was acting like that…."

She shrugged and smiled. "We all have our off moments, Cash. Sleep well," she said softly and left.

He returned to his room, thinking maybe a shower would soothe the savage beast.

***

Cash walked out of his bedroom straightening his tie at the same time Harper exited from hers. She blinked at the light. "Hey." Her voice was low from sleeping, and she looked a little worse for wear, to be truthful. Her hair stuck out everywhere. Somewhere she'd found striped pajama pants, a tank top, and fuzzy Wile E. Coyote slippers. She shuffled down the hall, yawning and stretching.

Ian already sat at the table his head in his hands. He looked up and grunted at Harper.

"Good morning, sunshine," she said, ruffling his hair.

"Stop," he responded like a petulant two-year-old.

She straddled the chair next to him and exhaled. Ian lifted his head a fraction, and slid a gigantic bottle of ibuprofen over to her, along with a glass of water.

She looked him straight in the eye. "I love you." She popped the top, poured out a handful, and downed them with the water. They folded their arms and laid their heads on the table.

Cash grinned, his heart warming at the sight. "Somebody not feeling well?" he asked loudly.

They both groaned.

Harper's muffled voice came from under her arms. "Is he always this chipper?"

Cash beat Ian to the punch. "Only when I wasn't in an unsanctioned shot war."

They raised their heads slowly and looked at each other. Then at him. Cash crossed his arms over his chest. "Ian. You were supposed to be watching out for Harper. If someone broke in here, you were completely useless in defending her."

Ian looked at Harper. She raised her shoulders, palms up, shaking her head with a perplexed expression. "He's right. I'm sorry."

"Okay?" She looked at Cash to see what would come next.

"But she started it," Ian couldn't help but add.

"I did start it."

"You're an officer of the law," Cash replied, not ready to let his friend off the hook.

Ian winced at his volume. "For God's sake, Cash. Have mercy."

The phone in Cash's pocket rang.

"My God. Even his *phone* is loud." He groaned as Cash fished it out.

"Cash Delmanaco."

"Cash. Hey. It's Ed Griesdeck. Homicide."

"Oh, hey, Ed. What can I do for you?"

"Well, Cap said I have a case that might interest you?"

"Okay."

"We hauled a...Jared Inglebrook from the water."

Cash's eyes snapped up and connected with Harper's. He took the call to the other room. "Where are you, Ed?"

"The waterfront. Near the Cooperstown Bridge."

"That's near like, the intersection of Fifth and High, right?"

"That's the one. They're doing construction on it. Have a lane closed."

Cash snatched the top of a bill from his desk and jotted the info down. "Okay. I'll be there in fifteen minutes." He hung up and ran a hand through his hair.

Not good.

Grabbing his jacket off the back of the recliner he headed to the door. "I'm taking off. You guys behave." He heard a couple of mumbled responses. He shook his head and smiled on his way out.

***

When Cash pulled up at the location, the tow truck was getting ready to leave with the waterlogged car. They were in an excavation company's parking lot, but the business had been closed for some time. The lot was massive, compared to the building, and Cash guessed that maybe some of the big equipment was kept on property. He got out of the car and rebuttoned his suit jacket as he walked as the breeze off the water was making it flap around too much.

"That was quick, Cash." Detective Griesdeck transferred the pad and pencil he was holding to his left hand so that he could shake with his right. "You even beat the M.E."

"Hey, Eddie. Thanks for calling." At his feet was a body covered with a tarp. Cash had seen too many of these kinds of crime scenes lately. He looked over his left shoulder at the bridge spanning the Buffalo River behind him, trying to orient himself to the scene. "So, he go over the side of the bridge or something? Maybe knocked out on impact?"

Eddie gave him an odd smile. "I don't think so."

Cash took in the location of the car and wondered what other scenario would land it in the drink. "Why?"

Eddie bent and lifted a corner of the tarp. "Because most drowning victims aren't wearing a noose around their necks. Looks like a hit." He stared at something over Cash's right shoulder. "What the hell is this now?"

Cash twisted to see what he was talking about. A cab pulled into the lot. His stomach dropped when he saw who got out of it. "Oh, shit. Cover it up."

Ed gave him a look, but quickly put the tarp back in place.

Cash moved toward the cab, trying to block her view, but he could tell by her expression it was too late.

"Is that Jared? That's Jared's car." With each word, her voice climbed the scale of hysteria. She tried to see behind him. "Is it him, Cash?"

By the time they reached each other, she was losing it. She tried to dodge around him but he intercepted, grasping her shoulders. She fought him, but she had to know the answer to her question. He braced himself and tried to keep her from the images that would haunt her for a lifetime.

She'd already had enough of those.

Her hand came to her mouth. She must have seen something that verified her suspicions. "No. Oh, no." She shook her head, wide, tear-filled eyes fixated on the bulge under the tarp. "No, Cash. It's him, isn't it?"

"I'm sorry."

"No. No." She beat his shoulders with her fists before collapsing into his arms. "Why?"

"Hey, lady. You gonna pay your tab? I don't have all day."

Really?

He helped her over to the Mustang and put her inside, glaring at the cabbie. Cash crouched beside her. "You stay here. I'll be right back." She didn't acknowledge him, simply stared straight ahead. Her body was providing the shock reaction that would make her numb soon.

"Hey." The cabbie was walking toward them.

Cash stood and closed the door, turning to face him and pulling out his wallet at the same time. "What's the fare?"

"Twenty-five bucks."

Cash stopped and scowled at him. No way did it cost that much to get here from his house. He handed him the cash then held out another bill.

"You've never seen her." He tilted his head in the direction of the car.

He licked his lips, eying the other bills in his wallet. "I don't know, man. Looker like her's hard to forget."

Cash frowned. "Look. Am I gonna have to give your license plate number to every cop in town to make sure you're following all of the traffic laws?"

His face fell. He snatched the twenty from his hand. "Fine. I've got amnesia."

Cash watched him walk away, then turned to peer through the window. She wore his Sabers hat and that silly scarf was wrapped around her neck. She'd taken a huge chance coming here, but at least she'd taken precautions.

What the hell was Ian thinking, letting her leave the house? And why hadn't he driven her himself?

Cash waved and called out. "Eddie. Thanks. I'll call you."

Eddie nodded, waving back. "Take care of whatever you have to."

Cash walked around the car, pulling out his phone and hitting speed dial before he climbed in. While it rang, he spoke to Harper. "It would make me feel a whole lot better if you ducked out of sight."

She looked at him blankly for a second, then drew her legs up on the seat and leaned to put her head in his lap, which looked god-awfully uncomfortable, even with his smaller center console, but he knew she was in a place where she wasn't feeling anything.

Ian picked up. "Hey. What's going on?"

"I was calling to see how Harper was doing?" He looked at her on his lap. Her cap was falling off, so he removed it and threw it on the floor board in front of her seat. She was glassy-eyed, her hands were palm to palm, stuck between her curled legs. How much could one person take?

"She's fine. Thanks for your concern about me, by the way."

He seemed pretty clueless. "What's she doing?"

"She went back to bed, which is where I would be if I weren't on guard duty here at the Delmanaco State Penn."

"Hmm. Could you go check on her for me, please? Make sure she's all right?"

He heard the chair scrape back. "I'm sure she's fine, Cash. She was in much better shape than me. The little shit. She's just—" After a slight pause, Cash could hear him calling her name, curious at first and escalating to frantic. He almost felt sorry for him. Almost. He stroked Harper's hair, and while it made him feel better, she didn't react.

"Shit." Ian was back. "She's not here, man. I can't find her anywhere."

"That's because she's here with me, you idiot."

"She's…" There were seconds of dead air, then he released a shaky breath. "Oh, thank God she's all right. I'm gonna rip her a new one when she gets back."

Cash had to smile at the contradictory statements. He started the engine. "No, you're not. She's had a bad enough day as it is."

"Why? Is she all right?"

"I'll explain when I get home."

CHAPTER THIRTEEN

Cash's tie was already off and slung over his shoulder with his jacket when he got home that evening. He expected to find Ian on the couch, but the living room was empty. He set a bag full of Mexican takeout food on the coffee table.

"Hello?"

"Down here."

Cash turned the corner. Ian sat in one of his kitchen chairs outside Harper's doorway, rocked backward so that only the back legs were touching the floor. His feet were on the opposite wall. He seemed engrossed in an issue of *Cosmopolitan*. He didn't look up until Cash grabbed the back of his chair and jerked it into an upright position, almost dethroning him.

"Look what you did to my wall, genius." Scuff marks from his shoes marred the paint, and he turned to see additional damage where the chair back hit the wall behind Ian.

"What?" Ian looked but waved it off. "Those'll come out. Did you know how pornographic the stuff is in here?" He held up the magazine and Cash snatched it out of his hands. He glanced in the room. Harper was under the covers with her back to him.

Ian twisted around, too. "We've established an open door policy. She won't be sneaking off on me again." He seemed proud of himself.

Cash managed to not roll his eyes. "Great." He stuck his hands in his pockets and nodded toward the bed. "How's she doing?"

"Better. She's speaking, which is an improvement from the catatonic state you brought her home in. She cried for a while, though. Broke my heart. I didn't like, know what to do." Cash nodded his understanding. "Maybe you should give it a try. I need a glass of water."

Cash leaned on the doorframe and continued to stare at the lump on the bed. "Dehydrated, are you?"

"You have no idea. Hey. Do I smell Mexican?"

Hearing the crinkle of the bag a few seconds later, Cash called out, "Don't eat it all." Ian's muffled response was no doubt given with his mouth around a taco. Harper stirred and rolled over. "Hey," he said softly. He laid his jacket and tie over the footboard and came to sit on the edge of the bed. He stroked her hair. "How are you doing?"

She gave him a faint smile. "Better." She worked her way to a seated position, the blanket falling in her lap. He could see she had on the Victory shirt she came in. "I'm glad you're home. I wanted to talk to you."

She fidgeted with the edge of the blanket and he got a sinking feeling.

"I wanted to see you and say goodbye in person."

He stood as if to distance himself from the concept. "Goodbye?"

"Cash. They…killed Jared because of me. They'll eventually come after you and Ian. It's not that I want to, but I don't see any other way around it."

The panic that he was experiencing made his volume increase. "Man. You sure have a lot of faith in my detective work."

"It's not that."

"So go out and handle this on your own. Is that your plan? Because it sucks." He threw his hands up. "You wouldn't last a week…a day, on your own."

Her jaw tightened and she glared at him. "I think I did pretty decent—"

"You were lucky. Damned lucky. And you won't be the next time."

Ian stuck his head in the door. "I heard yelling. Is everything all right?"

"Fine!" they both answered.

"O-o-kay." He retreated to the hall.

"You're so stubborn," Cash shouted.

"Well, you've got a little mule in you, too," she retorted, eyes flashing.

He looked away and set a closed fist on the brass ball on the bedpost. Talking about personality traits made him think of the Myers-Briggs test the entire police force had to take. The theory was if one could identify what type of person one was working with—whether fellow police officer, crime perpetrator, or a member of the general public—they would know what the best way to communicate with them was. If he wanted to convince her to stay, he had to use a tack that she would buy into.

She obviously cares more about other people than herself. Or she has a death wish.

He exhaled. "Listen, Harper. I'm sorry I yelled at you." He moved to sit near her on the bed again. "I was upset, but that's no excuse."

She looked away for a couple of seconds, then back. "I'm sorry, too. I just—" Her voice cracked. "I can't have anyone else I care for killed. I can't take it."

They both looked at her hands, worrying the cotton blanket. Cash covered them with one of his own. "I know. But honey, you are our only connection to the killer right now. If we lose you, there's a good chance he gets away with killing Kitty."

She flipped her hand palm up and held his hand. "And if I lose you, or Ian, or anyone else, I don't know if I can take it."

Frustrated, he laid his head on their hands and

groaned. When he lifted it he brought her hand to his lips and gave it a quick kiss. Then he covered it with his other hand. "Harper. We are trained police officers. Jared and Kitty were in over their heads."

"That doesn't mean the same thing won't happen to you."

He looked away and sighed.

I'll give it one more try.

He turned back and looked her in the eyes. "This man killed two of your friends. And he won't stop. We have an opportunity to put him in a place where he will never hurt anyone again. I asked you once to take a chance on me. You trusted me and it worked out, right?" She nodded rapidly. "Take another chance. Trust me. My experience, my training. I'll keep us all alive."

He held his breath.

A few tears snuck over her lash line. She looked away, staring at the window as if the blinds were open. Seconds passed. She lowered her head. "What do you want me to do?"

He exhaled, hanging his head, his neck and shoulder muscles relaxing little by little. He looked at her and smiled. "I need for you to look at those mug shots and find this bastard."

"Okay."

***

"Harper, you *need* to take a break. If you're not rested, you may make a mistake and click through his picture. And besides, if you don't eat these two tacos I warmed up for you, Ian will."

Ian folded the paper he was reading. "That's true."

She smiled. "Okay." Cash stood in the kitchen archway with a plate. "Thank you," she said as he handed it to her. "It smells delicious."

Since Ian was hogging the couch, she went around the

coffee table to sit in the recliner.

She was lifting the first taco to her mouth when she noticed an eerie quiet had descended. Cash was frozen in mid-stride between the kitchen and living room with a bag of Fritos in his hand. Ian was looking from her to Cash and back again. Without lowering the taco, she asked, "What?"

Cash shot Ian a warning glance.

She put her taco back on the plate. "What?" Ian stared at her, looked at the foot of the recliner, then back.

"Is this Cash's chair?"

Ian shook his head in a patronizing way. "Dude! Cash's chair is sacred. He prizes it above all things. Nothing comes between Cash and his chair."

Cash made an awkward shrug and came around to sit in the matching recliner opposite her. "She can sit there." He lowered himself stiffly into the chair.

Ian jumped to his feet. "What? You never let me sit there."

Cash plucked out a handful of Fritos. "You're not as cute as she is." He looked at her with a twinkle in his eye.

"What?" Ian said again, stamping his foot. "I'm damn cute. Aren't I, Harper?" He crossed his arms, leaning in Harper's direction and shooting Cash a smug grin.

When Harper continued eating her taco, he prompted, "Harper?"

She shrugged. "Sure. You're cute."

"See," he said in triumph.

Cash finished his bite. "You're still not as cute as her."

"What?" Ian's mouth hung open.

Cash put his arms out to the side, palms up, and tilted his head. "Sorry, man."

Ian snatched a taco from Harper's plate. "Give me that taco."

Cash opened his mouth, but Harper interrupted him. "It's fine. I can only eat one anyway." She leaned forward and whispered, "It's a consolation prize."

137

Ian huffed and stuffed a half a taco into his mouth, eating it in one bite, and dropping some shell on the floor. He grabbed his jacket. "I'm out of here."

Harper laughed. "Good night, Ian."

"Whatever."

***

Cash woke with a start. He listened. Someone was in the house. Ian left after devouring most of the take-out, and Harper had been in bed for hours. He had to tear her away from the computer, but she went to bed.

He grabbed his holster from the bedside table and quietly slid his gun out. He tried to identify the noises he was hearing, but couldn't. He crept out of bed and to the door. Taking the knob, he turned it slowly. He prayed the hinges wouldn't squeak. Taking a deep breath, he eased it open, soundlessly.

So far so good.

The hall light was off. He stepped out, his weapon raised. Harper's door was closed.

Good.

The living room was dark, except for a faint glow. He moved forward, the bluish light increasing.

No. It couldn't be.

He listened. *Click. Click. Click.*

He reached the end of the hall and his view widened. She was planted, a fist on the desk, chin on the fist, legs bent under her on the seat in what looked like an awkward position. Each click cycled through a page of mug shots. He stuck his gun in his waistband. He had to smile. Seeing her did that to him anyway. He never met anyone more determined than her. She was a strange mixture of tenderhearted and resilient, of sweet and cunning. A paradox that he loved to explore. As he passed the archway, he craned his neck to check the clock. Three-thirteen. He was afraid he'd scare her, so he purposely stepped harder to create a noise and alert her of his presence. At the same time, he softly called her name.

She spun around so fast he thought her head might go flying off. Her scream, if you could call it that, it was more like a beep, was piercing, as she brought her hand to her heart.

"Cash! My God. You scared me!"

He moved over to hug her. Her heart pounded right through her tank top and into him. One arm offered reassurance behind her back. The other hand was on the back of her head, drawing her into his stomach.

"Sorry." He drew back a couple of inches to look at her. "What are you doing?" He raised an eyebrow. "I thought I convinced you that you'd be much more efficient with a good night's sleep."

She pulled away, clumsily unwound her legs, and got to her feet. She looked at him, then glanced away, running her hand along the desk. She was stalling. Why? Her brow was furrowed, her mouth worked, but the words wouldn't come. He waited for her response.

"I tried to, Cash. I did." She turned her back and put several feet of distance between them. "It's just, sometimes when I close my eyes...."

"You have nightmares."

She swung around and stared at him.

"I woke myself screaming for years after my parents were murdered."

She nodded.

"Do you think it would help to...you know, have someone with you?"

She nodded again, and he extended his arm out to her. She slipped her hand in his and they went to her bedroom. He climbed in; she slipped off her sweatpants and slid in beside him. Curling up next to him, she laid her head on his chest. He wrapped his arm around her. At first he was hyperaware of her presence. The scent of her hair seduced him, the feel of her soft skin as she shifted and her leg came up on top of his, her warmth. But, after a bit, fatigue robbed him of his senses and he drifted off.

"Cash," she murmured.

"Hmm…?" He forced his eyes open but was surprised to find her still asleep, in the same position. He smiled and closed his eyes. But they popped open seconds later when he thought of Ian coming in and finding them together.

He carefully slid out from under her. She stirred, but didn't wake. Entering his room, he switched off his alarm clock, which was set to go off in less than five minutes anyway. He hit the shower and was coming out of his room when Ian arrived.

"Umm…." He pointed at Harper's door. "What happened to our open door policy?"

Cash frowned at him as he rapped his knuckles on Harper's door.

"Come in."

He turned the knob. "Good morning." The corners of his lips lifted.

"Good morning, Cash." She smiled. "How are you this morning?"

Ian looked from one to the other. "Wha-a-at's going on?"

They smiled wider and answered at the same time, "Nothing."

"Ri-i-ight. Anyway, Cash, check this out." Ian handed him a brochure. "We got this in the mail." As Cash read it over, Ian explained to Harper. "La Bonne Chance is holding a big gala tonight."

Cash looked up. "He'll probably be there."

Ian acted as if he was buffing a star on his chest. "My thinking exactly."

Cash began planning. "I'm gonna need to get a tux."

Harper piped up. "I'll go with you."

They turned to stare at her.

Cash blinked. "I'm going into the viper's den. Why on earth would I want to take you along with me?"

Her jaw hardened. "Because you're going into the viper's den, and I'm the only one who knows what the viper looks like."

"Not happening." Cash turned back to Ian. "You can rent shoes at those tux places, right?"

"I think so."

Harper folded her legs under her and leaned forward. "What do you mean, 'not happening'?"

Cash exchanged a look with Ian. "I mean you are *not* going." He turned again to his partner and opened his mouth, but before he could speak, Harper interrupted.

"Ian. Tell him what a fool he is to go alone."

Ian paused, looking into her face. "I agree with her."

Cash's jaw dropped open. "What?"

Ian held up a hand. "I don't like you going in by yourself either. It's too risky."

"I know, Ian. But what choice do we have? We can't let anyone else know about this until we know for sure who is involved. We can't trust anyone."

"You can trust me." He crossed his arms, looking hurt.

"You know I think you're the best wingman on the force. But I need someone to watch her." He gestured vaguely in Harper's direction.

"Umm. *Her* is right here. And you won't need anyone to watch me, because I'm coming with you. So if you two could get out of here so I can get dressed…."

Both of the men stepped into the room. They continued discussing their plans.

She tried again. "Then I could go with you and—"

"No!" they both barked. And Ian added, "Not happening."

"Fine!" she spat. She took hold of her shirt by the hem and whipped it off over her head.

Ian's eyes widened and a smile cut his face. "Holy shit!"

"Whoa, whoa, whoa!" Cash spun to block Ian's view,

waving his hands in front of him.

Ian tried to stretch around him to get a better view. Cash turned back and shoved him in the shoulders, trying to push him out the door. "Will you knock it off?"

"Cash. I'm a married man. I need to get my action where I c—Oh, my God."

Cash twisted his head back and Harper had slipped out of her pants, too. All the skin, the curves, the lace…. He was incredibly turned on, and at the same time frantic to cover her. Abandoning his struggle with Ian, he grabbed her and tried to fight her clothes back on.

"You're not going." It was like wrestling the wind. She slipped out of his grip constantly.

"Yes, I am."

"This is interesting…"

"Ian. Get. Out!" Cash was really losing his cool. "Harper. Stop acting like a little idiot." He was gritting his teeth so hard he felt like they'd turn to dust any second. He pushed her shoulders on the bed and had to close his eyes against the rising and falling of her breasts as she struggled against him. She lifted a knee, almost catching him in the crotch. "Hey. That was close!"

She wriggled beneath him. "Then. I'll. Aim. Better."

"You know what?" With a surge of strength, he fought her wrist up, reached for his belt and slapped cuffs on her so quickly she hardly seemed to know what happened. He locked the other end around one of the spindles of the brass bed.

He smiled down at her triumphantly. "You're not going." He shifted to again prevent her from racking him.

"Ooh. Kinky!"

Cash whirled around. "Will you get out of here before I have to come over there and teach you some manners?"

She jerked her hand, straining against the cuffs.

"Stop. You'll hurt yourself."

She screamed in anger and he jumped off the bed. He had to acknowledge, for a second, that part of him was aroused by the sight of her cuffed to the bed. Were circumstances different…. He wanted to reason with her, but she was flipping out. Beyond reason.

"Calm down. Please."

He left the room.

***

Harper fumed. Cash was going in there blind.

And I'm the idiot?

Her wrist ached where she strained against the metal cuffing her to the bed. She rubbed it with her other hand.

Not my best move.

Sulking, she tugged a blanket over her body.

Cash opened the door and stepped in. He stuck his hands in his pockets, grinning. "Good to see that you've learned some modesty."

She whipped off the blanket. He swallowed. She fixed him with the best come-hither stare she possessed. Licking her lips, she stretched out, shifting her body fluidly. "Why don't you come over here, and I can show you what else I've learned." She thought about adding "big boy," but decided that was a bit over the top.

His eyes lit up and he moved toward her with powerful strides. "And what would that be?" He sat beside her.

Her original plan was to lure him in and get another shot at his privates, but once he was this close, and she could catch the clean, slightly spicy scent of his cologne, her only thought was about how wonderful his lips would feel on hers. His eyes were so intense they lit a fire in her that had to be quenched. He leaned in a breath at a time. Her gaze flicked from his eyes to his lips and back again. She stretched to bring her mouth to his and drank him in. He tilted his head and drew her in deeper. Each kiss was a tug at her heart, roping her in.

"How come you get to kiss the handcuffed girl?"

"Get out," he growled, his lips still hovering near hers. He nibbled on her top lip and she resisted the moan that fought to escape her. "Did you really think," his voice was seductive, "you could get me into any position" he ran the back of his hand down the side of her face and she closed her eyes, "where you'd have a chance at racking me?"

Her eyes flew open. He was already at the door. He turned with a smile. "Thanks for the kiss."

The fury that spiked through her felt like it would blow through the roof of her head. A growl started in her chest and grew as it rose in her throat. She searched near her, snatched a vase off the bedside table, and flung it at the door as it closed. It hit, shattering in a fairly satisfying way. But the laughter coming through the door killed it.

He opened it and leaned in, shaking a finger at her. "Temper, temper."

The man is infuriating!

Minutes later, she heard the front door open and close, then silence. They'd left her. She looked at the handcuff chaining her to the bed. She had to go to that gala.

CHAPTER FOURTEEN

Whoever was in charge of the gala did a fine job. In some areas, an attendee might even forget they were in a casino. Scattered throughout one side of the wide-open lobby were high, circular stands covered in black cloths that twisted around the table's bases. Most of these were balancing the champagne flutes being handed out by waiters in black tails and waitresses in floor-length black dresses. They weaved in and out of partiers with round glass trays rimmed in gold, only big enough to carry four or five flutes at a time. Luckily, tons of them floated about, because Cash was damned well drinking his two hundred-dollars' worth, as that is what the tickets cost him. He snagged one from a pretty blonde and was raising it to his lips when he saw her.

She was walking away from him across the dance floor, but something about the tantalizing sway of her hips, or the delicious curve of her shoulder blades, or the store-bought but still beautiful color of the curls piled on top of her head, was sweetly familiar to him. Maybe his radar was too in tune to her frequency. He began to cut a path to her, throwing back his champagne as he moved and stashing his empty flute on the tray of a passing waiter. The distance gave him time to appreciate the way her dress fell away, exposing a large part of her back. The red in the sea of black and white was like a siren, although other guests also wore a variety of colors. It pissed him off. Might as well tie the noose around her elegant neck, which he noticed now did not look bruised.

Makeup?

As he stalked her, he timed his arrival, catching her up as the music swelled and twirling with her in his arms, one hand planted possessively on the skin of her lower back. Her sharp intake of breath satisfied him, but her scent sent a driving lust through him that he did not, at the moment, appreciate.

"What. The hell. Are you doing here?" She still seemed so shocked by his arrival that she was unable speak, although he enjoyed the way her inviting, painted mouth opened and closed with her confusion. "I could wring your pretty little neck," he growled in her ear, trying to ignore the way they fit together so perfectly and the way her body pressed against him, warming him inside and out. "How did you get away?'

"Those spindles on your bed unscrew."

Shit. Why didn't I think of that?

His gaze roved over her. Up close, he could now tell that the dress was more of a shimmery, metallic red. He didn't know if they'd call the sparkly stuff on the fabric sequins, but it certainly drew the eye like a flash of gold in a miner's pan. The material rose to collar her neck, and glided over hips, defining them with outrageous clarity. It was classy, not slutty, and sexy as hell. "The dress?" He raised his eyebrows.

She glanced away, wetting her lips. "I got it at a thrift shop."

He frowned. "With what money?"

She shrugged one shoulder, her face turning red. "Charlie let me write him an IOU."

I wonder what you agreed you owed him.

He clenched his jaw. "I told you not to come."

Her eyes shot fire. "You have no idea what he looks like. He could be dancing next to you right now, ready to shove a shiv in your spine."

146

It was a risk he was willing to take if he could end this nightmare for her. But right now, he had to get her out of there. Again he tried to determine what words would influence her the most. "Did you ever stop to think you coming here might be putting our lives in greater danger?"

Her eyes widened slightly, but she kept her chin high. "How?"

His concern for her fueled his anger. "Well, one, they could make you."

She shook her head. "They don't know I colored my hair."

He tilted his head. "Darling, any guy who's seen your eyes would never forget them."

This seemed to throw her. She lowered her head. When she raised it to search his face, her lips were trembling. "I shouldn't have come. I'm so sorry."

The concern on her face drained the anger from him. He tightened his hold and she laid her head on his chest. "Harper." He sighed. He raised his head slightly and Lewis DePesto was headed in their direction. A strange combination of panic and fury seized him. The anger he hoped to be able to take out on him at some point. The panic he needed to act on. And he didn't want Harper to see him. It would no doubt make her terror resurface. "Listen," he said quietly. "When this song ends we are going to casually leave the dance floor and head out the door. Okay?"

He felt her nod. All the fight had gone out of her. Lewis was closing the gap. Then Cash noticed Ian moving in a path to intercept the big man. He staggered and bumped Lewis, spilling a bit of his champagne on him. He made a big deal out of mopping him down, apologizing in a loud voice.

Ian laughed. "Wow. I guess I drank too much champagne."

A deep voice replied, "But we just started handing it out."

"I may have had some before we came here tonight," Ian responded in an exaggerated manner.

The music ended and Cash led Harper off the dance floor and out into the night, but not before he got a quick look at Lewis' face. His jaw was working back and forth. No doubt he was fighting to bite his tongue, knowing Ian was a guest.

When they hit the sidewalk, he immediately signaled for a cab.

"Cash. I should have listened to you. I—"

"We can talk about it when I get home. Take this for the fare." He shoved some bills into her hand.

"I'll pay you back for all this."

He opened her door. "I know you will." He wanted her as far away from the casino as possible, as quickly as possible. "I'll see you at home. Lock up when you get back." The last was probably unnecessary, but he felt compelled to add it anyway.

Closing the door, he took a step back. Through the glass he could see her hanging her head. It struck his heart.

At least she's safe.

The cab made its way out into the late night traffic and he watched until it was out of sight.

***

When he got back around twelve-forty-five she was waiting at the door. Still in her dress. She threw herself on him.

"Oh, thank God. I've been so worried."

"Hey," he said softly, throwing the tux jacket he carried in his hand on the couch and drawing her in against him. "I'm fine."

She leaned back to look up at him, then dropped her head, shaking it. "I don't know what I was thinking. I guess when I hear 'no,' I kind of go berserk. You're right. I'm stubborn." She lifted her face, peering into his eyes. "But this is no time to act like a child. This isn't a game. Lives are on the line, and I jeopardized yours and Ian's. I'm just not thinking clearly anymore. I should have listened to you. I should have—"

He put a finger to her lips. "Stop. Please." When she stilled and lowered her eyes, he lifted her chin. "I'm not angry. Ian and I are both fine. And the truth is," he glanced away, then back, returning his hand to the small of her back. "I should have handled things better. But *I* wasn't thinking clearly when you started taking off your clothes. In fact, I couldn't think at all."

Color suffused her face and she knit her brows, tilting her head and studying him. Her lips parted as if to speak, but nothing came out. She squirmed, hunching her shoulders and bringing her hands to smooth out the front of his shirt. "Really?"

He laughed. "*Really.*"

Her head came up quickly and she stepped back, glancing around the room. "The tickets were *so* expensive. I'll pay you back for that, and everything." She turned away and took a few steps over to the coffee table, picking up his uniform cap and brushing it off.

He studied her profile. "You've said that. Speaking of the tickets, how did you get in?"

She looked over at him, shrugging. "I told them my boyfriend and I got into a fight and he went in with the tickets, but he had my car keys and I couldn't get home."

He nodded, grasping the top of the recliner and leaning forward. "Believable." He was impressed.

She put the hat down, twisting to face him. "Besides, those things are kind of like ladies' night. They're more likely to let women in than men. Like backstage at a concert."

He moved forward, letting his gaze drop over her, heat rising from his toes. "That dress is really…something." The way it dipped in the back, her graceful shoulder blades, her hair done so prettily. He hadn't been able to stop thinking about her since the moment he'd seen her on the dance floor. Since the first moment he saw her at the blackjack table, actually.

She looked at her dress, brushing a hand over it. "Thank you. It is really pretty. I was surprised Charlie had anything that wasn't…"

"Slutty?"

She chuckled. "Yeah."

He continued to close the space between them. "Well, you look wonderful." That color blazed along her cheekbones again, making her even sexier. Everything she did was so…hot. "You know, this tux was pretty expensive."

Her eyes widened and she stuttered. "I-I know. I'm sorry. I'll—"

"Pay me back. Yes, you've said that. Repeatedly." He grabbed her hips, jerking her against him. "You can do something for me right now." He enjoyed how her eyes became even wider. The corners of his lips twitched.

"I can?"

"Yes. You can." And in an instant, he went from stalking predator, to weak-kneed. She had that power over him. The capacity to flip his emotional meter on its head. He wanted her, yes. But not in a way that was purely physical. "Dance with me, Harper." His voice came out surprisingly soft.

"What?"

The breathy way she said it had him dragging her closer. "Dance with me." He began to sway with her. Man, so tantalizing. The way their bodies met, and moved. To keep himself from losing control altogether he stepped back, took her hand, and raised it for her to twirl under. She looked at him intently as she slowly whirled and came back to him. His body was humming. He laughed a little and glanced away, and back. Never able to get enough of her. "God. You are so beautiful."

Her lips parted and he couldn't take it anymore. He brought his down and took hers, demanding more each second he breathed her in. She responded in a way that nearly undid him. She brought her hands to the side of his face as if to drag him in deeper, although he was far under the surface already. She stoked along his jaw, and continued to explore, her fingers coming between their lips, then sliding out to bury in the back of his hair. He trailed his mouth down her neck and she arched.

"Oh, Cash."

Her moan drove his muscles to tighten, the fingers that were clutching her drifting underneath fabric. So much skin. So much delicious, unbelievable skin.

She moaned again. "I need you."

And man do I need you! Every inch of me, needs every inch of you.

The blood drummed in his veins, pulsing with each beat of his heart. He'd kept apart from people since his parents' death. Participated in activities, sure. Entertained, and been entertained, yeah. But he hadn't felt, really felt, in a long time. It filled him with a sweet, aching pain. One he would never do without again.

She stumbled backward, leading her with him down the hall. She was taking him to the bedroom. He followed along but didn't have the patience needed to wait. He spun her and pressed her against the wall. A pleasured noise escaped her mouth. He felt her smile against his lips. She approved of his move.

But should he be doing this? She was emotionally vulnerable, and the race of his emotions scared him, too. Should he be losing his focus when she was in the crosshairs of some mobster?

Shut up.

Her teasing tongue brought him back to her. He wanted more of that. He stopped thinking and gave way to sensation. The heat of her thighs against him. The heady smell of her perfume, stirring him in ways he'd never experienced before. The arousing sounds of her moans coupled with the noise of hands traveling over bodies, and lips and tongues fueled by passion.

She eased her hands between them and gave him a

gentle push on his shoulders. He drew back, curious. She bit her lip, running her gaze along his chest, and bringing it back up again. In one smooth motion, she tugged off his already loosened tie then ripped through the buttons of his shirt. She yanked it out of his pants, skimmed her hands up the center of his chest and outward, pushing it to the floor. She put one hand behind her back, leaning against the wall, and crooked her finger at him with a laugh. He dove into her again, crushing her lips in a fierce kiss. She gave as good as she got.

When he came up for air, he opened his eyes. The cloth of her metallic red dress against her pale skin was a fire licking at him. It would only mean moving that material a couple of inches to make the whole thing fall at his feet, or so he thought. Kissing where fabric met skin he slowly pushed it off her shoulders. He leaned back to check out the way it fell, but it stopped at her elbows, revealing only the top of her black strapless bra.

He lifted his head. She was watching him. She gave him a slow, seductive smile, took his hands, and led them to a zipper in the middle of her back, running from above her hips to the tip of her tailbone. He glided it down while gazing into her eyes, a grin tugging his lips up. He slid his hands under her dress, his thumbs locked into the indention of her pelvic bone, fingers spread wide. Laying his forehead against hers, he took his time, savoring each millimeter as he traveled lower, over silky skin, to cup her ass. Their bodies sighed together and lips found each other again, this time with slow, deep kisses.

They were giving themselves to each other, and nothing would ever be the same.

She backed him away with her hips, stepped back with the room she'd created, and brought her fingers to grip the top of her dress. Understanding now, he took a step back. Maintaining eye contact, and taking a deep breath, she let the dress drop, shimmying until it pooled on the floor.

He couldn't move. Black lace, curves, man, was she built to perfection. Her eyes expressed her desire without her saying a word. Then they moved toward each other at the same time, her hands again going to his face, his diving under her ass and lifting her. She followed his lead, hopping and wrapping her legs around his waist, her arms around his neck.

Take her to the bedroom? Or continue exploring the possibilities out here?

He eased her against the wall. She moaned, seeming frustrated with the delay. He brought his head to her chest and slid his tongue along her skin.

"Oh." A purr rumbled through her.

She seemed to like the way this was headed. She tipped her head back and arched. One hand clutched at his head, tugging on his hair a little. The other she ran through her own hair and down her neck as she panted.

He kneaded her breasts, then yanked one side of her bra down and sucked on her nipple. She bucked against him and writhed, the sounds issuing from her taking a higher pitch. Yeah. This wouldn't last long.

He found her lips, pulled her off the wall, and took her to his bedroom door, bumping it open with their bodies. He set her on her feet and she immediately began to tear his belt off. The buckle jangled open, but she struggled with the pants button. He groaned.

"Oh, honey. You're killing me here." He took a step back, and slid the button through the hole, but before he could unzip she was there, urging the zipper down. He jerked at the cloth, trying to get the pants over his hip but froze when she slid her hands inside, closing his eyes. Oh, my God. It felt so good. She stroked him until he almost lost control, then glided her hands to his hips, shoehorning his pants off. When they fell, she dropped to her knees, wrapping her arms around him to clutch his ass. She switched, gliding fingers beneath his underwear and coaxing him to her mouth, her hot, wet breath seeping through his briefs.

No, no! Not yet.

He placed his fingers under her chin and coaxed her

153

up, kicking his pants the rest of the way off. Even though it was dimmer in the bedroom, with only the light pouring in from the hall, he could suddenly make out the bruising Lewis caused. He brushed the back of his hand along her neck, surprised by the swell of emotion that choked him.

The words spilled out of him. "I want to keep you safe."

She nodded, looking back and forth between his eyes and swallowing. "I know."

Pinching her chin gently between his thumb and fingers he tilted his head and kissed her gently. They quieted. What was all full of sexual energy and lust minutes before became serious. He put one knee on the bed, cradled her back, and eased her onto the mattress with his lips still on hers. He held himself over her in a plank position, wanting to absorb her beauty for a moment, and allow himself to feel what he was feeling for her.

She reached behind to fight off her bra and he, thankfully, had the presence of mind to retrieve a condom from the bedside table. When he turned back, her naked breasts left him speechless for a moment. He solemnly stripped off his underwear. The condom. This part was always so awkward. Before he had time to think about how best to handle it she sat, took the little package from him, smiled, placed it between her teeth, and ripped it open. He laughed.

"That was so sexy."

She grinned and he jumped when she grabbed him. Without looking away, she slowly rolled it on, and he held his breath, fighting for control. She walked her fingers up his chest and he came to her as she leaned back. Everything about this woman was perfect. He began to leisurely kiss her again, running his hands along the side of her body. He pushed away and let his eyes traverse over her again, then brought his gaze back up, brushing the hair from her shoulder. She pulled him on top of her and he adjusted so she could lead him inside her. Her eyes widened, then she sighed, arching her back and wrapping her legs around him. He rocked his hips, listening to her, aware of each tremble of her body, each innuendo in her movements, gaining knowledge of what pleasured her and memorizing it.

He'd never known it to feel so good to be buried in a woman, to drive his hips to hers, to watch the passion distort her face and bring her to the edge of bliss. Her frantic need for him fueled his for her. Fingernails raked across his back. He had no idea how he was hanging on, but he was definitely losing his hold. He wanted to stop. Take it back down. He tore himself away from her, but, like being stuck on vinyl, it stung him. He breathed hard, trying to figure out where to go next. She tipped her head toward the pillows.

"Go up there."

He wasn't sure what she wanted, but her hands were behind him, guiding him. She lifted a pillow and put it behind his back as he sat against the wooden headboard. In an elegant move he found absolutely mind-blowing she straddled him and took him in. Holding on to the top of the bed behind him, she began to move. He sucked in his breath, moving his hands to her ass so he could feel the way she rode him. He couldn't tear his gaze away from her. She was like some mythical goddess of bliss, rolling her hips and shooting a pleasure so intense through him he thought he would explode from it. The light from the hall kissed her body like an artist's brush painted her. He took hold of a breast and brought his mouth down, sucking hard, moving his hand to her back to support her as she cried out.

He wanted to affect her the way she affected him. To fill her with the phenomenal bliss she was sending coursing through his veins. He did what he could in his position to drive himself into her more fully, to meet her head on. He broke when she cried out and relaxed.

I have to have her now.

She shivered and let out a little sound of surprise and began to move again. Yes, he would give her more. He lowered her back to the mattress and she scooched back, giving him room to reposition himself. He got to his knees, grabbed her legs and wrapped them around him. He put his hands on the tops of her thighs and drew her into him more. Her breath quickened. He thrust into her, stronger with each stroke. Her cries came more quickly and he leaned forward, pressing his hands into the mattress as he continued to drive them both over the edge.

His arms and legs were shaking, and he could only imagine what she felt like.

"Are you…okay?" he managed to say between gulps of air.

"Mmm. Fine." She smiled with her eyes closed, looking both content and spent. He began to pull away but she cried out. "No. Not yet. Just a few more minutes."

He was more than happy to comply. But his arms wouldn't hold him any longer so he bent them and lowered himself on top of her, trying to hold as much of his weight off as he could. Several seconds passed and she relinquished, letting him go. She still gave a little cry of disappointment when he moved away.

"Come here." He reclined into the pillows and she bounced her way to him, snuggling under his arm. They continued to breathe and try to recover. He kissed the top of her head and squeezed her. He hadn't even realized how alone he was until she'd made him not want to be that way anymore. A deep peace washed over him. He wanted to tell her. Wanted to explain, but he had no words. He listened to her breathing become more regular, bending an arm to put it under his head. His body was like liquid, sinking into the bed.

CHAPTER FIFTEEN

Harper stretched. She felt so good. A touch sore, but more relaxed than she'd felt in her entire life. She smiled and opened her eyes. An unfamiliar ceiling hung above her, she frowned, trying to decipher where she was and becoming aware of breathing beside her. Cash! A series of explosive images from the previous night flashed through her mind. She smiled and turned over on her side, curling her hands underneath her cheek on the pillow. His face looked so peaceful.

The glare of the alarm clock cut into her vision.

Oh, shit. Ian!

She touched Cash's shoulder to wake him. Then she got caught up for a minute by what a big, solid shoulder it was. She shook herself and jostled him. "Cash?" He didn't move. She sighed, but her heart was light. It was probably for the best. If he were awake she'd want to make love to him again and they needed to make sure Ian didn't find out about that. He'd have a field day.

She flipped over and got out on the opposite side of the bed. An oxford shirt hung from his bathroom doorknob. She smiled and put it on, hugging it to herself and not bothering to button it. It smelled like him. She tiptoed around the bed and opened the door to the hallway to sneak across to her own bedroom but caught sight of her dress and his shirt and tie on the ground at the end of the hall. Again, she relived those moments in the hall. Those wonderful moments. She giggled and snuck down to pick them up. She opened Cash's door and threw the shirt in, and opened her own door to do the same with her dress. She needed a glass of water.

She turned and screamed, her arms flying out in front of her as if to ward him off, forgetting about her shirt, which parted. He stared, his mouth hanging open. No quick Ian quip came out of his mouth. He didn't even have the decency to look away. He just gawked. Heat rose from her toes. She whipped the shirt around herself with a squeak and dove into her room, mortally embarrassed.

***

Cash thought he heard a mouse, followed by a door slamming. He took in a deep breath and listened, but her scent distracted him. Harper. He turned toward her eagerly, but her side of the bed was empty. He felt the covers illogically, as if she might be hidden in its flatness. The sheets were still warm. Confusion and hurt swamped him. She was gone?

Slowly his mind woke. Ian. She didn't want him to know about them. And neither did he. Not until he knew what "they" were. He hopped out of bed and hit the shower. When he walked into the kitchen, Harper was sitting on a chair with her legs crisscrossed under her. She was blowing on a cup of coffee and Ian was staring at her with a weird expression on his face. Her head spun around when he entered and she jumped up, almost spilling her coffee.

"Hi." She grasped the top of her chair and wrung her hands around it. Ian cleared his throat and looked away.

He paused mid-stride, feeling like he'd walked in on something. "H-hi?" He looked at her and lifted his shoulders, mouthing, *What's going on?*

She shifted her gaze to Ian and back and scratched her

head, tilting it and giving it a slight shake before turning away, confusing him all the more.

Why are they acting so awkward? Did they have a fight? Or did Ian do something in appropriate again? His jaw tightened.

"Hey, buddy. How's it going?" Ian sang out, but he wasn't making eye contact. Cash felt like he'd stumbled across some bizarre alternate universe. He gave his head a hard shake and made a beeline for the coffee maker.

"Uhh...I'm going to—" Harper shot a look in Ian's direction and he dropped his head, focusing on his coffee cup, drumming his fingers on the rim. "—go into the living room and...yeah."

She backed out of the room. Once she hit the carpet, she scampered out of sight.

Cash leaned against the counter sipping his coffee and watching her strange exit, then whispered loudly to Ian. "What's up with her?"

Ian popped out of his chair, copying her movement by grasping the top of his chair and twisting his hands back and forth. "How the hell would I know?" A muscle along his jaw twitched. "Anyway, I've been thinking..." He zoned out, staring at the wall.

"Good for you, trying new things."

"What?" He looked confused, then caught on to the sarcasm. "Oh, yeah. Right. Thanks. Anyway, I've been thinking—"

"You said that."

"Okay. Will you shut up already so I can talk?"

Cash made a motion as if locking his lips and throwing the key into his coffee cup.

Ian scowled at him, but picked up his conversation. "We should probably think about moving her." He jerked his head in the direction of the living room. "She's been here a couple of days, and it's not safe to stay in one place long."

Cash nodded, all earlier discussion flying out of his head. "I've been thinking the same thing. What about my parents' cabin?"

Ian's face lit up. "That would be perfect. It's isolated. Not many people know about it..." He looked Cash in the eyes. "I think we should move her right away."

"Agreed."

"Cash. Ian." Her voice sounded odd. They both rushed into the next room.

She sat staring at the computer screen, but her posture was all wrong. Her shoulders slumped forward and she was shaking. They approached slowly and she turned. Tears coursed down her cheeks.

"That's him. That's the man who shot Kitty."

They leaned in, practically crowding her out. She put a hand over her mouth and sobbed.

He had a fairly good-looking face and curly hair, like Harper described, but the soullessness of his ice blue eyes commanded attention. "Alexei Ushakov," Ian read.

Cash's gaze flew over the page, soaking in each detail. "Brought up on everything from shoplifting to..." he reached for the mouse to scroll down the laundry list of charges, "money-laundering, marijuana smuggling, gambling and tax fraud, oxycodone distribution, loan sharking, labor union corruption, extortion, robbery, assault, assault, assault, murder..." He scanned the rest of the list silently, scrolling, scrolling.

Ian looked at Harper and put a hand on her arm. "It'll be okay. We're gonna get this guy. Make sure he doesn't hurt anyone again."

She nodded rapidly, flinging tears everywhere. She sniffled. "I need a Kleenex." She bolted from her chair and ran to her room. Clearly blowing her nose was an excuse to get some privacy.

They both turned back to the computer screen.

"Did you see how much time he's served?" Cash asked.

"No. How much?"

"Five months for two cases of tax fraud."

"You're kidding me." Ian read, trying to verify that information in the report.

Cash looked down the hall. "Witnesses seem to disappear come court time," he finished grimly.

Ian continued reading. "This is one bad dude." He turned to face Cash, the lines on his face tense. "We need to get her out. Now."

Cash nodded. "I'll go talk to her."

"We'll need to tell the captain, you know. This is beyond us."

He sighed. "I know. I'll go in after I explain things to her and you can run her out to the lake and—"

"No. I'll talk to the captain."

Cash's eyebrows shot up. He was going to face the wrath the captain would surely level out, knowing they had the location of the witness for days? Whatever happened between him and Harper must have been a doozy.

"I've been taking too many personal days to watch her. It might draw suspicion if I took another one."

"You can't talk to *anyone* else."

"I know. I won't. You just get her moved."

"I'm on it."

***

Harper didn't say two words on the entire drive. No, she said three. "I'm just tired," was the excuse she'd given for being quiet. He knew she was tired because he knew what they'd been doing half the night. But he also knew that wasn't what was bothering her.

Once at the cabin, Cash checked the cupboards and made a list of things for Ian to pick up when he came out. His phone vibrated in his pocket. Speak of the devil.

"What you got, Ian?"

"Hey. You guys get there safe?"

He opened the fridge, taking notes. "Yep. How'd things go with the boss man?"

"Better than expected. I'll tell you about it when I come out. Do you need me to pick up anything?"

"As a matter of fact..." He read through his list, adding a few more things.

"And what are the directions again? It's been a while since I've been out there."

Cash gave him the information and hung up.

"Do you have anything to drink?"

He was surprised to see her out of her room. "You mean like hot chocolate or something?" He set the list on the counter.

"I mean like tequila."

He came to her, massaging her shoulders. "Are you trying to get me drunk like you did Ian?" He grinned at her and was happy to see a slight upturn in her lips. "'Cause I'm not the lightweight that he is."

She tilted her head in a cute way, studying him. "I can take you."

He laughed. "Oh, really?"

She nodded, going over to the cabinets and opening the doors. "I won a lot of bets for Jared by—" She stopped and looked at him.

He swallowed and brushed his hand along the top of one of the upholstered kitchen chairs. "Go on."

She hesitated. "It's just...I could drink most of his friends under the table. They thought a tiny old five-foot-two girl like me couldn't—"

"Are you really five-two?"

She furrowed her brows, examining him in the kitchen's lights. "Yes. Why?" She crossed her arms with a frown.

"Oh, nothing. Go on. I'm sorry to interrupt."

She opened her mouth as if to say something, then turned and resumed her search of the cabinets. "He would bet them I could out drink them, and I would." She spun around, wielding a bottle of Don Julio. "Ta-da. Tequila." She looked at the bottle. "And good tequila, too." She reached back in and brought out two tumblers.

"We probably have shot glasses."

"This'll do." She poured some hefty drinks. "You wouldn't have any limes, would you?"

"No. And if I did, they'd be months old. I don't get out hcrc that often anymore."

She stuck the bottle under an arm and picked up the two glasses, nudging him on the way out to the spacious living room. "That's too bad. This place is incredible. I thought about saying that when we got here."

She curled up on the couch and he sat beside her. "So why didn't you? You were awfully quiet earlier." She handed him his glass, downed hers and began to pour another.

"Man. So much better than well tequila."

She sat back and he played with her hair, sipping his drink. He wouldn't get out of control with her. He needed to keep his wits about him. He wasn't foolish enough to think they'd made an arrest as yet. It would take time for the captain to put a team together quietly, which is what he hoped he was doing. He'd lectured Ian enough on the importance of that. He was anxious for his partner to get back so he could hear about what was going on with the case. It was good he didn't want to speak about things on the phone. He glanced over at Harper. She was swirling the tequila in her tumbler and staring into it.

"What are you thinking about?"

She didn't lift her head, but she stilled. Several seconds passed, and he about decided she wasn't going to share with him when she spoke.

"She didn't deserve that, you know."

She spoke as if he could hear the conversation going on in her head, but he knew who she was talking about. "What was she like?" he prompted quietly.

She laughed under her breath, raised the glass to her lips, and drank the contents like she was saluting her friend. Her eyes were teary from more than the booze. As she reached for the bottle to refill, she began to speak. "You would have liked her. I think. She could be brash, and self-centered, but…" She looked at him fully for the first time. "She was witty. Fun-loving." Her voice broke and she looked off to the side. She took a breath and seemed to be making an attempt to rein in her emotions. "Umm. She had bad taste in men, always losing her heart to guys that were using her. She was seeing someone when…it happened, and at first I thought it might be the guy who shot her."

Cash shifted uncomfortably. If she only knew.

"She was the life of the party. The spotlight was always focused on her." She shook her head. "But boy could she make it shine."

She took another drink, but he was happy to see she was slowing. She crossed her legs under herself facing him directly. He had his near arm stretched over the back of the couch, one foot on the floor, the other bent casually, its ankle resting on the knee of the other leg.

"I was the quiet one. The solid one. Dependable. But Kitty tried."

She took another swig. So much for going slow.

She chuckled again. "We met in the second grade. My parents and I moved to St. Louis from Kansas City, my dad switching from Hallmark to Anheuser-Busch. He's in marketing," she explained. She exhaled, but a big smile was lighting her face. "Kitty came up to me on the playground—I was painfully shy at the time. Only child. I never had many friends growing up. Before Hallmark, we'd moved to Kansas City from Rochester where my dad worked for Eastman-Kodak. Friends were hard to come by when you moved a lot. Sure, you were a subject of interest as the new girl, for a while, but kids would eventually return their attention to their real friends and you were left in the dirt. I guess I wasn't all that interesting."

"I doubt that."

She drank, nodding her head and wiping the back of her hand across her mouth. "No. It's true. I was a bookworm. Books never fail ya." She poured. "Do you want some more?"

"No. I'm good."

"Nerdy girls aren't attractive. Nerdy guys, yes. Nerdy girls, no. Anyway—"

"I'm disagreeing with you on that one." He rubbed her hand. "I think nerdy girls are hot." She looked him straight in the eye and that flash of heat she always gave sizzled through him.

She smiled. "I haven't kissed you all day."

"No, you haven't."

She leaned forward and brushed her lips over his. The taste and scent of the tequila on her was pleasant, arousing. The kiss that followed shot straight to his groin. His mind went to images of her in that dress, them against the wall, her in his bed…. He wanted to repeat that encounter now. New walls. New beds. But Ian would be here soon. They agreed he would spend the night in the guest bedroom. Harper was in the master. Cash couldn't sleep in his parents' rooms, either here or at the house.

Still, her pulling away was like ripping a Band-Aid off. "How long 'til Ian gets here?"

He put a finger to her mouth, tracing her lips. "Too soon for me to do even a fraction of the things I want to do with you."

"Mmm."

Her fantastic blue eyes sparked wickedly and he almost added, *We could get a few of them out of the way….* But He knew it wouldn't be enough for him.

She got up, taking her drink with her to the wall of windows behind him. It was floor to ceiling glass, peaking at the top like the roof. It was his favorite feature of the cabin, and perhaps hers, too. He twisted to watch her. Was it necessary for her to put distance between them, too? In order to behave? She planted a shoulder against the glass, staring out into the darkness.

"Anyway, I got kind of distracted from my story," she looked at him meaningfully and desire speared through him again, then she returned her gaze to outside. It was usually beautiful out there, but this early in spring it was still mud, dead grass, and leafless trees. The lake was pretty, of course, but he doubted she could see that far in the dark. When he brought her back the next time, they could take long walks, and fish. Was he thinking about a future together?

She continued. "Kitty came up to me that first day on the playground and said, 'Hi. Do you want to be my friend?' We were like peas in a pod from that point on. She even followed me and Jar—"

"You can talk about him. I'd be a fool to think you weren't in any relationships before."

She walked toward him. "Actually, Jared was the only one."

This stung, although he wasn't sure why. She came around the couch and sat beside him with a sigh. "Jared was kind of a lost soul. Estranged from his family. He was kind of a drifter before we met." She sat lost in thought for a moment. "I think I was more of a mother to him than anything else, although he was much older than me." After another brief pause, she added, "I walked in to him and a hooker on my couch."

He was cheating on both of them.

"He shouted out, 'I'm not paying her,' which he somehow thought made him blameless in my eyes." She shook her head.

Cash put an arm around her. "I'm sorry that happened to you."

She shrugged, but cuddled into his side. "Worse things have happened to people. I've never been shot or had a rope tied around my neck before. Not yet, anyway."

"Hey, hey." He put a fist under her chin and lifted her face. "We won't let that happen."

She studied his face. "Why do you care? Why do you care what happens to me? I'm just a dealer you met, and you're risking your life for me."

"Well, to start with, I'm an officer of the law, so it's

kind of my job. And secondly, I've come to care about you a great deal." She ran her hand across his chest, smoothing his sweater out. Of course, it would be hard for her to trust a guy again, after what she'd been through. "And…I know last night was pretty…spur of the moment, shall we say?"

She smiled at that.

"But…I don't do that lightly. I haven't been with many women, and I've never let anyone in." They were quiet for a moment. "I've rarely talked about my parents' death before, and then, only briefly. But I wanted to tell you."

She lifted her chin to look at him. "Thank you."

He was reminded of that time at the blackjack table, when she was so close and he wanted to kiss her, before they'd even introduced themselves. Now that he had kissed her, he didn't think he'd ever get enough of it. He lowered his lips to hers, pulling on them, drawing her closer. She put a hand on the side of his face, and things began to heat up.

"Umm, excuse me."

They jumped apart.

Ian was juggling grocery bags as he came in the door. He seemed irritated for some reason. Cash hopped up. "Let me help you, buddy."

"Yes. That would be nice." He scowled at Cash, giving him a meaningful look, but the meaning was lost on him.

What did Ian have to be pissed about?

Cash took one of the bags from his hands.

Harper stood and turned, her cheeks blazing red. "Need any more help?"

"Nah. We got it," Ian responded in a slightly nicer tone.

"Okay. Well, I'm showering then. Cool with you gentlemen?"

The thought of that body with water running over it stopped Cash's brain from functioning. And apparently Ian's, too. Ian recovered first, jabbing him in the ribs with an elbow.

"Sure."

"Fine," they said at the same time.

She shuffled off, eying them warily.

When they were in the kitchen, Ian kept shooting him looks, but didn't speak. Finally, Cash stopped putting groceries away and asked, "Did I do something specific to piss you off, or is this just a pissed-at-Cash kinda day?"

"What do you think you're doing?" he hissed.

Cash looked at the peanut butter jar still in his hand. "Putting away groceries."

Ian smacked his arm.

"Ouch."

"That's not what I'm asking. With *her*?" he said in an exaggerated manner, gesturing in the direction of the bedrooms. "And don't act like you don't know what I'm talking about."

"I won't have to act like I don't know what you're talking about because I haven't a frigging clue."

He put his hands on his hips and Cash felt like he was being chewed out by an angry spouse. "She's vulnerable right now. She freaking watched her best friend get blown away and saw her boyfriend's body being—"

"Ex-boyfriend."

"*Ex*-boyfriend, whatever. A guy she still cared about's body being towed out of a watery grave with a noose tied around his neck."

Cash wanted to deny he knew where this was leading, but he couldn't. At least internally.

"All this I know."

Ian punched him in the shoulder again, this time harder.

"Ouch. What's your deal?" Cash rubbed his shoulder.

"You can't take advantage of her when she's weak."

"Ian. You're blowing this out of proportion. We—"

He was seriously pissed. Yelling at him. "Oh. And you weren't macking on her when I walked in the door?"

"Macking? What are we, twelve?"

"I certainly hope not."

Cash let out a breath. "Ian, she's a big girl. She knows what she's doing."

He threw his hand up. "You know she doesn't have her head on straight right now."

Cash leaned against the counter. "Actually, I think she's doing a remarkable job."

"Well, I do, too. But that's not what we're talking about."

"Well, I wish to hell I knew what we *are* talking about."

"Wait a minute…. That's why I saw her naked in the hall! She was coming from your room wasn't she?"

Cash straightened to his full height, bristling. "You saw her naked in the hall?"

Ian's mouth hung open for a moment. "Let's not change the subject. You slept with her, didn't you?"

He tried not to let anything show, but apparently failed.

"You did!" He turned around and took an angry spin, coming back to where he'd started. The vein was pulsing near his temple, a sure sign he was about to explode. "How could you?"

Cash huffed, guilt gnawing at him. "Come on, man. You saw that dress."

"Don't tell me you're victim shaming right now."

"Victim? Victim? She was a perfectly willing participant in last night's activities. In fact, more than willing," he couldn't help but gloat.

"Spare me the lurid details," Ian spat.

"Wait a minute. Are you, Ian Tate, lecturing me about how to treat women?"

He colored.

No witty comeback for that, brother?

"I just don't want to see her get hurt." His anger dissipated, leaving him deflated.

Cash still held on to a scrap of anger. He saw her

naked? "Well, neither do I, pal."

Ian leaned forward with both hands spread wide on the counter. "Fine."

"Can we talk about the case now?"

Ian pushed off the counter. "Whatever floats your boat."

"What did the captain say?"

"You mean before or after he chewed my ass out?"

Cash was about to apologize for putting him in that position, but he went on.

"He's put four units in the woods around here. One more at the mouth of the drive coming in here."

Cash nodded. "Good."

"He called the US marshal's office to get the Witness Protection stuff rolling."

"Witness protection?"

"Yeah." Ian stared at him. "You didn't think you'd get to hang around protecting her forever, did ya?"

He hadn't thought about it at all. A ball of ice began to form in his stomach. When he didn't speak, Ian continued.

"He started assembling a task force—" before Cash could say anything, he held up a hand, "—on the down low. He's pulling in people from other areas. He may even reach out to the Buffalo PD. The bust may go down as soon as tomorrow, depending on how quickly the marshals get things in order."

Cash slumped against the refrigerator. "Who did you see there?" he asked dully.

"At the precinct?"

Cash nodded. Ian understood what he meant. Was anyone acting strangely? Maybe unintentionally tipping them off that they were on the mob's payroll?

"Let's just say I was imagining punching a whole lot of guys I never wanted to punch before. Eddie Griesdeck was there. Tommy Mallory. Uhh…I saw Mike Beason. He was picking Dr. Hayashi's brain about where he thought Harper might be hiding. Chump. Uhh…oh yeah, I saw Dick

Wainwright. Haven't seen him for a while."

"Nothing unusual?"

"Nah. Same ol', same ol'."

"Okay. Good."

Cash turned and continued to put the peanut butter away. So they'd almost gotten her to the finish line. But what would happen to them after she crossed it? The thought began to consume him.

CHAPTER SIXTEEN

Cash lay on top of his covers in pajama pants, his arms crossed behind his head, watching the shadows of tree limbs dance on the ceiling. The wind buffeted the branches and howled around the house. Wind advisories were out, but no talk of rain. But the weather wasn't what was occupying his mind.

It had been an uncomfortable evening for poor Harper. Cash had remained stone silent. Ian had spent the time brooding. No wonder she went to bed. She claimed that tequila made her sleepy, but it was obvious she'd wanted to get away from them.

How could he have ignored the fact she would be put in Witness Protection and whisked away from him, never to be seen or heard from again. He'd been so focused on keeping her safe he had left himself open to be blindsided.

Maybe this was how things were supposed to turn out. A brief fling, then they'd go their separate ways? He flipped on his side, punching the pillow to fluff it. Maybe a bit harder than necessary. The more he thought about it, the more that didn't seem right.

He realized in an instant of rare clarity that he needed her in more than the physical sense. The night his parents were killed, a hole was created in his life. He was able to patch it in the weeks and months following, but it was like that cold patch stuff they used on roads for stopgap measures. It might buy some time, but eventually it wears away, and the hole is still there. His infrequent forays into the dating world were the same. He dated some nice women, had some very pleasant physical relationships, but they never filled the hole. Not even close. She made the ache go away, and he didn't want to lose that.

Maybe it's time to give up this whole hero thing. Maybe I can be a hero to one person. Maybe it can be her.

He was probably getting ahead of himself.

Ian was right.

Is that even possible?

Yes. He was right about it being wrong to take advantage of her during a crisis. But he wouldn't have time to win her over to his way of thinking. Everything might be over as soon as tomorrow night. He wanted to be with her tonight. Tell her goodbye, if that was how it had to be. He swung his legs over the side of the bed and was about to stand when a board squeaked in the hall. He reached for his revolver on the nightstand, but the door opened.

"Cash?"

"Harper, what's wrong?"

Her silhouette shrugged. "I don't know. I can't sleep. Maybe it's the wind. I keep thinking I'm hearing things outside."

"Come here."

She closed the door and ran to the bed. He smiled, holding up the covers to let her in. She slid beneath the sheets and turned her back to him, pressing herself along his side.

"Geez! You're cold."

"I guess I've been waiting out in the hall for a while. Trying to decide whether I should come in."

He moved hair away so he could plant a kiss behind her ear. "I'm glad you did."

She flipped over to face him. "Okay. The truth is…I wanted to be next to you. I'll sneak out in the morning before Ian gets up."

"And risk him seeing you naked in the hall again? No way."

She gasped. "He told you that?"

"Yeah, he told me that." He pushed onto one elbow. "And I told him—" He slid his hands under her tank. "—that no one gets to see you naked except for me."

She giggled, then stilled as he brought his hand to cup her breast, brushing his thumb over a nipple. Thinking better of it, he brought it to her stomach, rubbed it for a few seconds, then flopped on the mattress, staring at the ceiling again with his arm resting on his forehead.

"Umm…. What was that?"

He was so confused. He twisted and pushed back onto his elbow. "Harper. Am I taking advantage of you?"

She made a clucking noise. "No."

He skimmed his fingers over her arm. She put her hand on his to stop it, then brought it to her lips, kissing it. "Cash. You've given me something I've needed. Something I've needed for a long time, but convinced myself I could do without. I've felt so alone. Even when Jared and I were still together." She found the side of his face and caressed it, grazing his lips with her thumb. "I don't feel as lonely anymore."

He leaned down and took her lips, flipping to lie on her partially. He pulled away, but Harper kept her hand in his hair, playing with it. His hand drew circles on her stomach. "You know, when they bring Alexei Ushakov in for questioning, they'll put you into the Witness Protection program and take you somewhere far away from here. I'll never be able to contact you again." She stilled.

"I won't let them."

"I'm not sure you'll be given much of a choice. And besides, it is the safest thing to do."

She pushed up on an elbow. "And I won't see my folks again?"

"I don't know. I don't know how all that will work."

She flopped back onto the mattress like he had, laying

her arm across her forehead. "That bastard." He could tell she was crying. "It wasn't enough to kill Kitty and Jared, he had to friggin' screw up my entire life." She began to sob.

He slid his hand under her, lying down. "Come here." He held her close, kissing the top of her head. "We'll figure it out. Don't cry." She wept against his chest for a while and he whispered comforting things, but he was full of dread.

After a bit, she stopped crying. He trailed his fingers up and down her arm in a soothing fashion, but neither spoke. He thought she fell asleep and was surprised when she kicked her leg over him and rose to straddle his pelvis. He couldn't see her face in the dark, but he could make out enough to know she ripped her tank off over her head and threw it somewhere.

"What are you doing?"

"If they are going to take you from me tomorrow, I'm damned well showing you how I feel about you tonight." She proceeded to trail kisses down his chest, rolling her tongue along his stomach and began to work off his pants. He lifted his hips to give her clearance and she stripped off all his clothes in one fell swoop. Before they even hit the floor her mouth was on him, doing such incredible things he would have screamed out were Ian not rooms away.

"Oh, God, Harper." He laced his fingers in her hair. During a moment of excruciating pleasure, he accidentally tugged on her hair, and she seemed to like it, so he dug in deeper. She seemed to know when to slow things and exactly how to take him to the edge. In the midst of one of these calmer, but still intense moments he took the opportunity to take her by the shoulders and flip them both.

"My turn," he growled. He explored every inch of her incredible body, then explored some more, learning to read her every sound and move. They made love well into the night and were so tired the thought of what they might have to face the next day couldn't keep them awake.

***

One moment their world was silent. The next it was a battle zone. A tremendous crash was followed by shouts, thuds, and the cracking of things being destroyed in the living room. It took seconds to even understand what was going on, having woken from a dead sleep. Cash slid on his pajama pants.

"Cash! What's happening?"

"I don't know. You stay here."

"You're not going out there?"

"I'll be back," he whispered, trying to reassure her. He opened the door a crack, trying to gage where the intruders might be. Ian showed up in the doorway across from him. Bare-chested like him. No Kevlar. His revolver his only weapon. His face was determined but concerned.

It became clear they were hearing automatic rifle fire. *What the hell are they shooting at? No one's even out there.*

Ian shouted over the chaos. "We need to get down the hall. Engage them away from her."

Cash nodded, although walking the gauntlet of the hall was an intimidating prospect. Nowhere they could dive for cover. But in seconds they'd be charging the hall anyway. Keeping their backs to the wall, they made their way without meeting anyone. Cash chanced a quick look around the corner. He wasn't prepared for what he saw. Seventy-five percent of the glass in the windows were shot out. The couch was riddled with holes and feathers from throw pillows floated lazily down despite the pandemonium surrounding them. The wind whipped in from the hole that was his parents' living room wall, swirling around and bringing in leaves, twigs, and other debris.

At least six men wearing black clothing and ski masks stood in position, spread about like hockey players playing zone defense. They held AK 47s and AR 15s—along with several automatic rifles he didn't recognize—like they were hockey sticks. A shot blew a hole in the wall opposite him, feet from where Ian stood. They were outmanned and outgunned.

Where the hell was the cover the captain said he supplied? Four teams and no one was aware of the automatic rifle fire erupting in his living room?

Ian came to his side of the wall. They simultaneously attempted to exchange gunfire, Ian going low when Cash went high. Cash was happy to see, and sort of terrified to see, at the same time, that they were being effective. Each took out one player. But when they swung around the corner the next time, two more stepped through the opening—where jagged pieces of glass still hung like manmade stalactites—replacing the assailants who went down.

They conserved their ammunition, but both guns ended up clicking empty at the same time.

"Shit!" Ian summarized. "What are we going to do now?"

Cash nodded to the opposite side of the living room.

"Your dad's gun case? You'll never get there."

"I've got to try."

"I can't offer you any cover, man. I'm out of ammo."

"Yeah. I know. Just distract them or something."

"What the hell do you want me to do, perform a striptease or something?"

"That'd work." He switched to the wall across from them, holding up three fingers, then two. At the next interval, he went, running low and diving behind the couch while bullets shattered the lip of the counter separating the kitchen from the dining room. He put an arm up to protect his face from shrapnel, be it bullets, or pieces of the wood flying around. He didn't have to worry about breaking the gun cabinet's glass front. They'd taken care of that for him. But as he picked out a rifle, he was hit by a memory.

He was at a happy hour, talking guns with Mike Beason.

"At my dad's place on Lake McCoy he's got a gun cabinet filled with his old Marine sniper equipment."

177

Beason tilted his head. "Lake McCoy?"

Cash nodded. "It's a private lake out Route Five."

He shook his head. He needed to think through that conversation, but now was not the time.

He took out a rifle and spun it across the floor to Ian. Then a revolver. He grabbed two guns for himself and spun ammo to Ian. The box fell short of his reach.

Cover me, Ian mouthed.

Cash loaded and went over the top of the couch, taking aim and hitting two men. They might not be assault rifles, but as a Marine sniper, his dad's M40s had unparalleled accuracy. Hopefully the quality of their shots would counter the quantity of their attackers. Ian had retrieved his ammo and was loading. Cash was surprised they weren't being rushed, but he'd take any breaks he could get.

He was about to pop over the top of the couch again when a piercing scream rent the air. His blood turned to ice.

Harper!

Ian was already running down the hall. Cash went up and took a handful of shots before taking off at a run, and barrel-rolling when he got beyond the couch. Bullets whizzed and pinged all around him but he had only one thought—Harper's safety. Once he hit the hall he scrambled to his feet. Ian kicked the door to his bedroom open. She was still screaming. Ian cursed, falling against the wall and grabbing his shoulder. He'd been hit. Cash's eyes widened, but Ian stepped up to take a few more shots. Harper's screams were becoming more distant.

Ian's words came to him in slow motion. "Cash! Get down!"

A bullet hit his arm and he tripped over his feet. Ian took one shot and a thump told Cash a body fell behind him. He didn't take time to look. Staying low he kept running. Ian continued to shoot at targets aiming at Cash's back. When Cash reached the doorway, his momentum carried him into the frame, hitting it with his injured shoulder. The bullet only grazed him, but it still stung like hell. He winced, but entered the room. A huge figure in black was dragging Harper by her hair across the room. She was still on her feet, trying to fight her hair out of his grip, but Cash could see he had a large hunk twisted around his arm. Noting his entry, the man put his massive free arm around Harper's middle, lifting her off her feet, effectively both moving her in the direction he wanted and using her as a human shield. She thrashed about, kicking and beating her fists into his massive arm, trying to jar herself free. Cash didn't see the shooter until it was too late. He was crouching behind the window they blew out, the barrel of his gun steadied on the sill. The flash of the muzzle was the only warning he got. He dove over the bed. The lamp on his bedside table shattered.

"Cash!" Harper's scream was heartbreaking.

"Shut up, you stupid bitch, or we kill you here."

"Cash! No!"

He tried to get to his feet, but he was tangled in the sheets. She was crying now. She thought he was hit. He army crawled to the end of the bed. Harper was putting up one hell of a fight, but the man hauling her made it to the window and hands lugged her through. He didn't have a clear shot, but if he could get her attention and get her to duck….

"Harper!"

She lifted her face and made eye contact. At the same time the man holding her let go of her hair and landed a blow to the side of her head. She went limp. Cash's heart leapt, but he kept his cool, leveling his revolver to take the now clear shot. The big guy fell, but they were already guiding her unconscious body through the opening. He started to stand but was forced back into cover by the shooter in the window. He had the best position and better weaponry. The gunfire around him began to peter out. A shot rang out from close range. The barrel aimed at him jerked up, firing into the ceiling. Cash lifted his head. Ian stood inside the doorway with his gun still pointed at the window. Several vehicles started outside.

"Where is she?"

"They've got her. Come on." Cash stuck his gun in his back waistband as he came around the bed. Pushing glass aside, he got his keys off his bedside table. "We've got the Mustang. We can catch them. Are you okay?"

"Yes. A damn chunk of the door was buried in my shoulder, but I pulled it out and it feels a lot better. You?"

"Fine. Come on."

They went out the front, out the non-window, not bothering with the door. They ran to the Mustang. Cash stuck keys in the door.

"Cash."

He peered over the roof of the car as he opened the door. "What?"

Ian's head was down. "They shot out the tires."

With dread, he lowered his gaze. He beat his hand on the roof.

Four cars raced down the lane, sirens blaring. They screeched to a halt and Mike Beason got out of the lead car.

"We thought we heard some gunfire."

Cash was marching toward him.

"You okay, Cash? You're bleeding."

Without any prelude Cash landed a whopping right to his jaw. Beason went down on one knee. Ian ran over.

"Cash. Stop. It's not his fault they have her."

"Who? The girl?" Beason asked, spitting out blood. He stumbled to his feet. Men poured out of cars and gathered around, unsure of what to do.

Cash grabbed Beason by the sides of his jacket and threw him against the car. "Where are they taking her?"

"How the hell would I know?"

"Wrong answer." Another right rocked him.

Mike held up his hands. "Cash, buddy. I think you're losing it."

"Where are they taking her?"

"Get your partner under control," Beason barked. "Before I lose my patience."

Cash took a step back and delivered to his ribcage. He

doubled over, coughing.

"Cash," Ian warned.

He turned his head. "He's the only one who knew about this place!" he shouted.

Ian looked at Beason, who eyed him warily and straightened, breathing hard. Ian's eyes turned cold and he clenched his fists. "When you're done, I want my turn."

"Oh, that won't be necessary." Cash again grabbed fistfuls of Beason's jacket, yanking him away from the car, and slamming him against it. He took the gun out of his waistband and held it to Beason's temple. "I'll give you one last chance. My old man's gun is pretty outdated, and it's been known to misfire."

The nearest officer drew his weapon, aiming it in Cash's direction. Ian squared up to him, planting his feet wide as he pulled his Colt .38 out and spoke to him. "Do we have a problem?"

"No." He jerked his head toward Beason. "He had us stand guard at 'the wrong cabin,' then led us on a wild goose chase."

Realization seemed to dawn on his partner's face and he, too, produced a gun, pointing it at Beason. The distinctive sound of Cash's gun being engaged grabbed everyone's attention.

"You've got about five seconds," he said through gritted teeth, his chin jutting out.

Beason's body slumped and Cash seemed to be holding him up. "Okay, okay." His gaze darted around the gathered circle, from one man to another. He licked his lips. "Alexei has a private airfield."

"Where?"

"Used to be Spirit Airport."

Ian spoke up. "I know the place."

Cash released Beason and took a step back, knowing the other officers trained their weapons on him. "You better not be lying." He headed around the front of Beason's unmarked, which he never turned off.

Ian approached the passenger's side, staring at the traitorous cop. "Get the hell out of my way."

Beason stepped back, but a bit of fire returned to his eyes. "He kept the girl alive as a guarantee." He looked over at Cash with a grin, blood showing between each tooth. "As soon as they're underway, he's gonna kill her. If she's lucky."

Ian swung and connected with a roundhouse. Beason went down. "Boys," he said to the other officers as he opened his car door.

"Yeah. We got this," one answered as they closed ranks around the snake.

***

Cash gunned the motor, taking the car in an incredibly tight angle over grass and gravel alike to turn it around, before roaring down the lane. When he hit Route 5 he opened up the engine, testing its limits.

Ian planted a hand on the dash. When Cash didn't slow and went screaming around a curve he shouted, "Easy, Cash! You're like a man possessed. I don't want to lose my life because you have the hots for Five-Foot-Two."

It was nerves talking, and Cash knew it. "It's not like that."

"Then what is it like?"

"I think I'm in love with her."

Slowly a smile crept over Ian's face. He flipped on the lights.

CHAPTER SEVENTEEN

Harper moaned, rocking her head. Ropes cut into her wrists and ankles, and the seat she was tied to was hard. She was cold, and she realized that all she wore was one of Cash's shirts. The voices came to her like in a dream.

"Why don't we just kill her now?"

The next had a Russian accent. "Do you think if we kill her they'll stop chasing us? She's our insurance. Whenever the pilot is done getting this *damned* airplane ready," he shouted the last, "we'll get out of here."

A hand lifted her chin. She blinked her eyes open, but the light was so bright it stung. She was in a huge, wide-open building. A rolling tool box stood to her right and she could hear the clang of metal on metal behind her. The man who shot her best friend loomed over her.

His voice managed to be gentle and creepy at the same time. "Until then, she stays alive."

She shook her head, trying to clear it and get his hand off her at the same time. He crouched in front of her, rubbing her knee. "It's too bad you had to see us kill your friend, but she refused to work for me, be one of my girls, to pay off her debt." His eyes roamed over her and goose pimples rose on her arms. He talked slowly now, using his tongue a lot. "What about you? I bet you'd bring a fair price." His hand roamed up her inner thigh.

She lurched away from him, almost toppling the

chair. "Get your freakish hands off me!"

His eyes turned hard. He straightened to his full height, towering over her. The backhand he dealt her did knock the chair down. She groaned, laying helpless in his shadow. "Get her up," he said as if bored.

The chair was hauled upright and he was in her face. Lewis DePesto. "You're a hard woman to kill, sweetheart." He plucked the letter opener that she's stuck in his chest out of his inner pocket. He rubbed the tip along her jaw, looking at it, then at her, grinning. "But this'll do the trick." He licked the tip of the opener and she was hit with a wave of revulsion. His eyes shone. Jutting out his chin he added, "I've been waiting for you."

Alexei Ushakov stood with his back to them, his arms behind him, one hand circling the wrist of the other. He twisted his head slightly so his words would be heard. "Quit playing with her."

Lewis stared at Alexei's back, his face tightening, but he did what he was told.

"You're like a big guard dog," she hissed at him. "Doing every single thing your master says."

Lewis looked at his boss. Alexei nodded. The next backhand knocked the chair over, too, and her head smacked on the concrete. Her ears were ringing, but she still heard the siren.

Alexei whirled around. "Untie her. Quick." Four men appeared from somewhere to her right and behind her, marching toward a massive door on one end of the building Gunshots rang out. Lewis disappeared behind her. Without warning, her arms were jerked up and pain coursed through her. Her scream of agony only seemed to turn her tormentor on. She heard the pop of cartilage and cried out again.

"Hurry up. Get her to her feet. Don't bother with the arms."

The ropes around her ankles tightened even more and they began to throb. The tension from the sawing action going on behind her increased her pain. Alexei had a gun out.

Was it the same one that shot Kitty? A barrage of gunfire came from the area where the men exited.

One siren. Her heart sunk. *It has to be Cash. Doesn't he realize he's fighting a losing battle?*

The rope gave and fell on top of her feet. The blood rushing to her toes was excruciating. Hands clasped her arms, bringing her roughly to her feet, which wouldn't bear her weight at first. The whir of what seemed like a thousand sirens penetrated the metal walls of the building and hope gathered in her chest.

"Close it," Alexei barked to someone. She twisted her head. A man in blue coveralls stood under a small plane wielding a tool of some sort. A hatch was open above him.

He wiped his hands on a rag he produced from somewhere. "But I'm not done."

Alexei strode toward him, gun raised. "Yes. You are."

The man held up his hands. "Okay, okay." He swung doors closed.

Alexei twirled, marching back with a determined expression. His ice blue eyes penetrated her, filling her with terror. She broke away from Lewis but only got a few feet away before he snagged her again, dragging her back to the plane. She fought with everything she had in her. If she could stall long enough, help would come.

Alexei reached them and slapped her. He bent to get in her face, spitting as he talked. "You *will* cooperate."

"Like hell I will."

He grabbed her opposite arm and both men dragged her toward a staircase leading to the door of the airplane. They reached the foot of it and panic seized her. Once through that doorway she was no longer needed. Shouts filled the air. Cash and Ian were the first ones in. Navy VPD T-shirts graced their chests, but they were still shoeless, Cash in pajama pants, Ian in sweats. Men swarmed in behind them wearing Kevlar and tactical helmets. A lead man pointed each man in different directions and they fanned out, finding cover behind barrels, stacks of tires, rolling staircases,

185

forklifts, crane looking things, and anything else that would conceal them.

She found energy to renew her struggle to free herself, surging forward and straining against her captors. If anything, it would slow them. They returned fire with their free hands, making it difficult to restrain her.

Lewis took a shot. "Son-of-a-bitch!" He put his hand to his shoulder and brought it away, covered in blood. "Now I'm pissed." Illogically, he marched into gunfire. He took aim at an officer on some scaffolding and Harper screamed when he fell to the floor. Alexei changed his grip, wrapping an arm around her middle. But he wasn't as strong as Lewis. Harper planted an elbow to his ribs and broke free. She headed toward the nearest crate. When she was within feet, a bullet hit it, splintering the wood top. Her hands still tied, she slid on her side to cover.

She worked her way to her feet and squatted behind her shelter. The crate was the perfect height to keep her out of sight. She searched for Cash, or Ian, or anyone on the right side of the law, but no one was close. She duck-walked to a crate behind her, turning so that her hands were against a corner. She moved her hands up and down, trying to use the rough wood to saw through the rope. Her wrists and the sides of her hands were getting scraped and filled with splinters. She sucked in air but moved her hands all the more quickly.

A tremendous explosion knocked her off her feet again. A bullet pierced a barrel of something flammable and it was engulfed in flames. Similar barrels were lined up within feet of the first.

This whole place is going to blow!

✳✳✳

Cash peered around the corner of a forklift and took shots at anyone wearing black. In the back of his mind, he worried about crooked cops ambushing him from behind. Harper said two of the men who shot Kitty and chased her were at the station, so Beason wasn't the only one. Then again, maybe the renegade boys in blue were wearing black tonight and fighting on the bad guys' side. He eyed his target. If he was to reach the crate Harper had disappeared behind, he would first need to leave cover and reach a trash can about three feet away. He ran low and shot at random to his left, making it without problem. Luckily, his side of the hangar wasn't seeing much action at the moment. Next, a barrel about the size and shape of the one that had exploded. For a second he flashed back to his younger days in the school cafeteria where he would jump to the "safe" red tiles in the ocean of white ones. What he'd do to be back there now.

But he needed to get Harper safely out of this battle zone. He ran to a crate about four feet away, but angled so as not to provide much cover. He reached it, and made it around to the other side where he was more protected. He took a second to assess the situation. She was around here somewhere, but with dozens of crates, which one concealed her? To his right he spotted one of the mobile staircases that could be wheeled out to planes. If he could get higher, he could see behind all of the crates. At the same time, he'd be totally exposing himself. He decided a quick peek was worth the risk. He had climbed only three steps when he spotted her. At the same time, he noticed Lewis DePesto on the other side of the crate he'd abandoned, with his gun trained on an unaware Harper, who'd managed to free her hands.

Without much thought, he launched himself in DePesto's direction while screaming out her name. He didn't clear the crate. In fact, he belly-flopped pretty much directly on top of it, but it was enough to distract Lewis. His momentum carried him over the side of the crate and he came crashing down on his target, wrapping his arms around Lewis's neck.

Lewis growled and tried to dislodge him with a shake, but Cash held on like he was riding the mechanical bull at the Buckin' Buffalo Saloon on a bet. A huge paw grabbed his shoulder and threw him to the floor.

Uh-oh.

Lewis held a gun to his temple.

"Are you the son-of-a-bitch that shot me? 'Cause I wanna kill the son-of-a-bitch that shot me."

Cash knew there was no winning answer to that question.

"Maybe you'll do, thou—"

Harper used the only weapon she had left to her, her bare feet, kicking the gun out of Lewis' hands. He lunged at her, grabbed her ankle and upended her, hard. Cash landed a jab to his ribcage, but in such crowded quarters, he couldn't get much behind it. Lewis was intent on Harper, who was trying to scramble away, on her back. The *smack* of flesh meeting flesh was followed by a cry from Harper. He was pinned by the big man's weight. Cash lost his gun when he decided to take flight from the stairs. He located it within a foot of Harper, but her terrified eyes were on Lewis, who was reeling her in like a fish.

"No! No!" She kicked out at her attacker, but he only secured the other ankle, making it easier to drag her in.

"Harper!"

She looked at him and he nodded toward the gun. She turned her head and spotted it, snagging it as Lewis reached her knees. She swung it around.

"Let us go!" Her hands were shaking like crazy, but at this close of range, there'd be no missing him.

Lewis froze, momentarily. He narrowed his eyes. "I can't do that."

"Shoot, Harper!"

He laid a meaty hand on her bare hip and was able to draw her in further, almost close enough to reach the gun.

"Shoot!"

She closed her eyes. Three shots rang out, one after the other. Lewis DePesto pitched forward onto Harper's legs. His head was twisted to the side, eyes wide open. He gurgled and blood came out of his ears and mouth. Then he was still.

Ian stood on top of a crate about ten feet away, his

legs out wide, gun still pointed at Lewis. Harper, trapped under Lewis, looked like she was going to be sick. Cash pushed the lower part of the body off his legs and crawled over to Harper, putting his arm around her.

"Hey, baby. I've got you."

She was a mess. She clung to him, sobbing and shaking and pretty much incoherent.

I guess that's what happens when you watch a man die on top of you.

Ian sprang like a mountain goat from crate to crate, then down to the floor next to them. He crouched to look at Harper with pity for a second without saying anything, his own eyes wet. He raised his gaze to Cash.

"I had to do it, man. He would have killed her." His thoughts shifted back to Harper and he ran a hand along her hair. "But this is so wrong." His voice cracked.

Cash put a hand on his shoulder and he glanced up. "You saved her life. You saved both of our lives."

He closed his eyes and nodded. When he opened them, he seemed to have it more together. He peered at Lewis. "We have to get her out of here. This place is going to blow."

Cash got to his feet, put his hands underneath Harper's arms and locked them around her chest to try to drag her from beneath DePesto's body. Ian did what he could to help. When she finally was free, she looked at Lewis' blood all over her legs and screamed again, fighting them as she turned to get away from it.

"Hold her." Ian bent and put his arms around her, trying to calm her.

Cash whipped off his VPD shirt and tried to mop the blood off her. It was still warm and that, with the smell, was making his stomach roll. He threw the shirt down and put one arm behind her back, slipping the other under her legs and was about to lift her when a second barrel exploded. He threw himself over her to prevent any debris from falling on her, shrugging off whatever fell on him. Heat licked at his bare back and the temperature of the room skyrocketed. He scooped her up.

"Go! Go! Go!"

He and Ian ran, dodging around the hangar paraphernalia and steering clear of chunks of twisted burning metal and wood. Thick black smoke rolled in waves from the epicenter of the explosion out. A couple of yards from the door another blast about knocked Cash off his feet. He stumbled, but righted himself, coughing, but quickening his pace all the more. Ian ran ahead to open the door. When they stepped through, they were surprised to see the sky was lightening. They made sure they were clear of the building by quite a distance. Fire engines and ambulances were pouring onto the grounds. Police officers stumbled out of the building. When mobsters did, they were immediately arrested. The earth under their feet shuddered with the next chain reactive explosions. Balls of fire burst out the doors, every window was shattered, and columns of flames shot through the roof. The heat was intense, even from fifty yards away.

When Cash tried to get medical help for Harper's abrasions and head trauma, she clung to him, refusing to let go. No amount of convincing could get her to loosen her grip. The EMTs suggested a sedative, but when they wrestled her arm down to inject it, Ian went ballistic.

"What the hell are you doing? Don't hurt her!" When she went limp a few minutes later, he questioned the amount of drugs they used. "Where did you get your EMT licenses from anyway? Beauty school?"

Cash and Ian got to ride along in the ambulance as their injuries needed to be assessed, too. The men sat on either side of her, bent forward with their forearms on their knees. The EMT fiddled with her IV. Minutes passed. Harper looked so pale, her bruises the only thing giving her color. Cash took her hand.

Ian broke the silence. "How can you stay so friggin' calm?"

Sensing an accusation lurked beneath his words, Cash snapped. "Maybe because I friggin' realize that cussing out the people that are trying to help Harper isn't the best choice."

They stared at each other heatedly until Ian looked away.

"They didn't have to be so friggin' rough," he mumbled.

Cash looked at the EMT and rolled his eyes.

When they arrived at the hospital, it was decided that all Cash needed was to be cleaned up and bandaged. Ian's wound required stitches.

Cash stood by Harper's bed with his hands stuck in the pockets of the scrubs he was given. The monitors beeped a reassuring beat, but he still wished she would wake. He was incredibly tired and still trying to wrap his mind around the fact that hours ago he was holding the woman he now knew he loved, and all hell broke loose. His parents' living room was a shambles, he'd beaten the crap out of Beason, which was one of the highlights of the evening, and add to that all the shit that went down at the hangar, and it was a bit to take in.

Harper began to whimper and thrash her head from side to side. Cash pushed a button by the bed, but no one came.

"No! No! Please, no! Cash!"

"I'm right here, honey." When holding her hand wouldn't calm her he glanced over his shoulder. Seeing no one out in the hall, he lowered the rail of the bed and climbed in with her. She quieted, but tears continued to squeeze out of her closed eyes. He didn't realize how much he needed her comfort. She looked so lifeless. But lying next to her he could feel her heat and it eased his mind.

At some point, Ian entered. He didn't say anything, just sat in a chair on the opposite side from Cash. Probably fifteen minutes had passed when he startled Cash by saying, "That was friggin' intense."

Cash laughed. "You are the master of understatement."

Ian smiled, but looked at his folded hands. "The captain said Alexei Ushakov died in the fire, along with most of his cronies."

Cash absorbed this. His forehead wrinkled. "The captain was here? Why didn't he stop in?"

Ian peered into Harper's face. "We decided not to disturb you." A few minutes later he put in. "The sellouts were Rick Ryder, by the way, and Nicholas Spritzhammer."

Cash arched his brows. "Rick Ryder?"

"I know. I friggin' went fishing with the guy."

"That's your new favorite word you know, friggin'."

"It's a good word."

It was quiet again. Cash brushed the hair off Harper's face. "It's over you know. With Alexei dead, there's no need for her to testify. No testifying, no threat."

Ian chuckled and reached between the bedrails to run a finger over Harper's hand. "I'll miss our little motley crew." He sat back. "Plus, now I've got to go home to my kids."

"Ooh. Chrissy's going to be so pissed when she sees those stitches."

"Or turned on." Ian wiggled his brows like Groucho Marx.

"You wish."

They were quiet again. Cash thought about what he'd said. No testifying, no threat. No threat, no need for protection. No need for protection, no him? He contemplated what that would mean to him.

CHAPTER EIGHTEEN

As it turned out, having a man take his last breath at her feet trumped both watching her best friend be murdered, and seeing her ex-boyfriend's body removed from the swamp, in the traumatizing department. Harper had been plagued by nightmares for months. At the beginning, she spent nights with Cash. But she felt she needed to face things herself and moved to a hotel. She couldn't stay at her apartment anymore. She'd spend a night at Cash's here and there, but he hadn't seen her in over a week. And when she called to ask him to dinner at her hotel this evening, he was filled with dread.

Despite that, Cash couldn't help but be excited about seeing her. He missed her. She made his life better. When the maître de asked him if he wanted to sit outside on the cobblestone patio or in, he changed his mind three times, finally settling on a table inside near the door to the patio, which was left open. He checked his phone. He arrived early, which made her being late more painful. It was an absolutely gorgeous evening and Cash ordered a beer and watched tiny birds dance around the feet of patrons sitting outside. He willed himself not to check the time, but did anyway.

She's not really that late, when you take into account the fact that I was early.

Three beers in, he was sure something was wrong.

She wouldn't call to ask him out and not show, unless she'd been in a terrible accident, or her room caught fire, or something. He loosened his tie a bit. He was finding it hard to swallow.

When she finally showed, he realized he hadn't been taking full breaths for a half-hour. He exhaled and jumped up. "Hi!" He slid her chair out for her. She looked fantastic. She'd dyed her hair back to almost its natural color. Her therapist said it would help her forget the On-The-Run-For-Her-Life Harper, and remember the semi-well-adjusted Harper.

"Hi. I'm sorry I'm late." Her voice was flat and without energy.

No explanation?

When Cash returned to his seat and got a good view of her, his palms began to sweat. She wasn't looking at him. Deep circles were formed under her eyes, like she hadn't slept since the last time he saw her. Which she probably hadn't. Her eyelids were puffy and her makeup was washed away. She'd been crying.

He decided his best tactic was to ignore all this and fill their conversation with pleasant talk. But it was hard to have a conversation with someone whose mouth seemed to be unable to make a word beyond one syllable. Her leg bounced like a coke addict going through the DTs. She'd almost spilled her water twice. He told her some funny stories about Ian and his new baby, and he was awarded a couple smiles for that, but they were short lived. He was running out of conversation by the time the waiter brought the bill and handed it to Harper.

"Wait...what? I've got dinner."

"No, you don't," she insisted. "I owe you for all the meals I've eaten at your place. And there's this." She slid an envelope across the table.

Cash leaned back in his chair, tilting his head and not touching it. "What is that?"

"For the gala tickets and the tuxes and stuff."

He twisted the stem of his water glass. "I'm not taking it."

She blinked and looked away, not saying anything. He had to talk. He had to say something to make this awkwardness go away. "Hey, I know you love hockey. I got tickets for us to the season opener."

"Cash, I'm leaving tomorrow," she blurted out with a slight stammer.

He leaned forward, in a full panic now. "What do you mean?"

"I'm," she chanced a quick look at him, then studied the curtains behind his back, "I'm going back to St. Louis." Now she'd gotten started, everything came rolling out so fast he had a hard time understanding her. "I don't belong here anymore. Kitty's gone. Jared's gone. Everyone I knew worked at the casino, and I'm sure the hell not going back there. Nothing's left for me here. I need to start over."

He captured her hand on the table. "Harper. Ian has a sister who's a pediatrician. She's opening a private practice and needs a receptionist. I've already talked to her about you. She—"

"Oh, Cash. I can't. I just can't." She stood and ran out the door. He should have thought about that. Don't supply an escape path.

Throwing his napkin on the table, Cash rose to follow her, almost running into the waiter.

"We'll be back. I swear."

At least she didn't get far. She stood at the edge of the patio with her back to him, dabbing her face with a Kleenex she must have dug out of her purse.

He took her elbow. "Harper, I—" Not here, too many people were around. "Come with me, please."

He led her around a corner to an alcove where a fountain sat, a mermaid spitting out water in the middle. "Harper, please. You do have something back here, or you can. I want you to stay." She shook her head rapidly, but he went on. "I want you to stay. I want to be with you." He still held her hand. "Listen, I asked you once to take a chance on me. I'm asking you again. I promise, I won't hurt you like Jared did. I will prize you above all things and nothing will come between us. I swear with my life."

He didn't know what else to say. He hoped he said things the right way. That it was enough.

She gazed into his eyes for the longest minute of his life then nodded.

"You'll stay? You'll give us a chance?"

Her eyes glistened and she smiled in the most beautiful way he'd ever seen. "Yes, Cash."

He took her in his arms, exhaling and releasing all the tension he'd been carrying around in his body the whole day. He closed his eyes. "I love you. And I'll make sure you don't regret taking that chance."

CHAPTER NINETEEN

EPILOGUE

"Do you mind?"

The player in the chair to his left stared pointedly at his foot. Cash was rhythmically kicking the table with it, and had apparently been doing so for a while. He grimaced, sitting straighter in order to move the offending foot away from its target. "Sorry."

He glanced over and caught Harper's lips twitching as she dealt the next hand.

Amused, are you?

It warmed his heart and he took a deeper breath, relaxing his shoulders and arm muscles. They had been dating for the last nine months, known each other for over a year now, and she was his everything. He wasn't afraid to admit that.

He'd been surprised, shocked, really, when she told him she was going back to work at La Bonne Chance. But her therapist encouraged her to do whatever she needed to in order to feel more in control of her life. And, he had to admit, it made the perfect setting for what he was about to do.

Harper's hands waltzed along the green felt, delivering cards to Joe, then Ian, then him and the guy

197

next to him. He thought about those hands and how—when he'd stolen a kiss from her in one of the outer hallways on her break—they'd fanned out over his chest and along his arms, her long nails creating heat and friction wherever they roamed. His heart beat quickened all the more as he remembered what those hands, and the rest of her, had done to him the night before, in a hotel room a few floors above their heads....

Ian cleared his throat and Cash plummeted back to Earth. He scanned the cards on the table, and raised his gaze to Harper's. One of those havoc-wreaking hands hesitated at the mouth of the shoe. She threw a look at the guy to his left. He was preoccupied with a waitress who'd stopped to take his order. Harper leaned in, her captivating eyes peering over his shoulder in the direction of the bar.

"I know you're off the clock and not eying any beautiful blond suspects at the moment, so what has you so distracted?" she hummed.

To his right, Ian and Joe were involved in some discussion over how Ian should have played his last hand.

"Uum...blondes, no." He smiled, moving closer to her and lowering his voice. "But I do have a thing for this one redhead...."

Her lashes fluttered and she dropped her head, a rosy blush blossoming along her cheekbones. It was a huge turn on.

A shadow fell across the table and Cash hurriedly signaled for a hit, then waved off another card. While Harper was occupied with the next player, he locked eyes with the towering Asian pit boss behind her. Cash learned his name was Aran Chen when he'd talked to him earlier. The man's gargantuan arms were crossed over his chest, the severe tightness of his ponytail making his face seem even stonier than usual, his gaze hard and calculating. Without changing expression, Aran winked. It happened so quickly, Cash wasn't sure if he'd imagined it or not. He slid his hand into his pocket, fingering the object within. He ran his thumb pad over it then flipped the item end-to-end several times.

He sighed. It was now or never. He pulled it out, pushing it, and all his chips, into the betting circle. Harper busted. She clinked a small column of chips next to the stack in Joe's circle, matching its height. She paid Ian and came to his pile. She froze, blinking and staring at the sphere of gold resting on top of his chips, the attached diamond sparkling in the casino lights.

Slowly she raised her head. Tears were in her eyes, but her expression seemed almost pained. As tall as he was, Aran Chen stretched to see over her shoulder. Harper had her arms held wide as she gripped the edge of the table, her mouth pressed together. Cash licked his lips and looked again to Chen, who gave a slight nod. Movement had stopped around him, voices coming to a halt mid-sentence.

"Shit!" Ian summed up pithily.

Cash's heart thumped against his ribcage like a caged bird. "Harper. Umm. I'm not sure exactly how to say this…." His mind went blank.

Ian nudged him. "Well, make some attempt, man."

Cash ran a hand through his hair. "I had this all worked out," he mumbled, searching for the words he had so carefully ordered in his head throughout the week.

"Just tell her how you feel," Ian urged. Cash turned his head to glare at him.

Joe clamped his hands on Ian's shoulders. "I think he's got this."

"I don't know, Joe. He seems to be

struggling."

Cash tuned him out, swallowing and turning to face Harper again. Her lips were trembling and she brought a hand up to cover her mouth as she stared at him with round eyes. Suddenly he felt completely calm and clearheaded. "Harper. You are one of the strongest, most compassionate women I know. In fact, everything you do seems to amaze me. I—"

"She is pretty amazing," Ian commented.

Cash didn't even turn. "Joe?"

Ian's garbled "What?" escaped from behind the hand Joe slapped over his mouth.

Cash stood, but he didn't feel like they were close enough. He glanced at Chen. "May I?"

The big man nodded his head rapidly and gave Harper a little shove to the right. Cash snatched the ring off the top of the pile and ran around to meet her at the end of the table, taking her hand. "You've filled up a hole inside me and made me feel real, solid, again. You gave me back the capacity to love." He gave his head a shake. "I never knew that I could love someone so much. So…." He lowered himself to one knee.

"Nice touch!" Ian's commentary was silenced by Joe and Aran's shushing.

"I want this to last a lifetime." He smiled. "So, baby, I'm *all in*," he said the last slowly, reverently. "Say you'll marry me, Harper, and make me the happiest man on the planet."

"Yes," she said, and not waiting for him to slide the ring on she pulled him to his feet and threw her arms around him. Cheers went up as they kissed.

"Thank God. I was getting nervous." Ian frowned at Joe. "You knew about this?"

The older man grinned. "Hadn't a clue."

Chen patted Cash on the back and shook his hand. "I did."

"You told *him*?" Ian turned to Cash, seeming hurt.

"I had to. I wasn't exactly making your standard bet." Cash spotted someone in the crowd. "And of course they knew."

Ian turned as a couple rushed forward.

"Mom! Dad!" Harper wrapped them up in an embrace and all three began to bawl.

Ian pulled out his phone. "I've got to tell Chrissy. She's been pulling for this since the first night she met Harper." He moved off to find a quieter area.

Cash stepped back over to Harper. She parted from her parents and embraced him. "You brought my parents here?"

"Well, of course. I needed to ask your dad's permission in person. So I—" The rest of his statement was smothered in a kiss.

Chen raised his hands over them. "We have some winners here, folks."

Everyone clapped again, and Cash shifted to dip his fiancée. He'd definitely lost his heart at La Bonne Chance, and it was the best thing that ever happened to him.

Note from author

Thank you for reading TAKE A CHANCE ON ME, part of my REAL ROMANCE COLLECTION. I hope you enjoyed it. Now that you've read the book, won't you please consider writing a review? Reviews are one of the best ways readers discover great new books. They don't need to be fancy or long, just a sentence or two honestly describing your opinion of/experience with the book.
I would sincerely appreciate it.
Want more from M.J. Schiller?

Page forward for
an excerpt from
TO HELL IN A COACH BAG
Book One in the DEVILISH DIVAS SERIES

TO HELL IN A COACH BAG

CHAPTER ONE

Danielle

Sure, Hell was stamped on my passport, but I was ready for a change of scenery. It was time for me to put the past behind me and move forward.

On the other hand, after losing my husband, I'd been carrying around my grief for so long my arms were like spaghetti. A new fire may have started to burn inside me, or, at least a glimmer of it, but would the strength it took to begin my life again be equal to the desire to do so? This was the constant debate taking place in my head.

"Hey. You okay?"

I twisted to find my gal pal, concert buddy, and fellow lunch lady, Samantha, staring at me. I sat beside her in her ex-husband's convertible as we whizzed down the highway on our way to Chicago and the All State Arena. I'd agreed to attend a Chase Hatton concert with her. I'd be getting myself out there. Maybe that was a start.

And the two of us always had fun together. In fact, our coworkers often told us we were going to Hell in a handbasket. If that's where I was going, I had the best travel partner ever. The thought gave my spirits a boost. I flashed her a smile. "Absolutely."

She grinned. "Now, that's more like it." She switched lanes without bothering to signal, earning us a honk, and the honker a one-finger salute. "Lighten up," Sam muttered. She drove barefoot with her left leg crossed over her right casually like we were at a slumber party not on a highway going—I glanced over—eighty-five miles an hour. Good lord!

I had to shout over the wind to be heard. "Why on earth did Bill agree to let you have his baby this weekend? He knows how you drive."

She glowered at me. "Very funny, Dani." She

zoomed past a school bus, a sedan, and a pickup truck before cutting over again. "I told him he owed me. He ruined my life."

She waved those four little words around like a color bearer did the flag in battle. It had gotten her many an expensive bauble. "I still don't get it. I wouldn't put up with all the grief Bill gives you even if he bought me a whole fleet of these convertibles."

She shrugged. "He's my kids' dad."

This always shut me up, and she knew it. *If I'd caught my husband in bed with—never mind.* I wasn't Sam and I couldn't begin to understand their relationship as I had, thankfully, never been there before. I let the subject drop, relaxing back into my seat and closing my eyes to Sam's creative lane shifting for a bit.

It was a beautiful early spring day. One of those days where the starched white clouds hung from the sky like clean laundry on a clothesline. Behind us, snuggled into the back seat, were two of the best little concert signs poster board and permanent marker could make. In a sea of people, signs helped you to stand out. They read, "Lunch ladies heart Chase Hatton!" and "We have access to government meat!"

It was our running joke that doors would open for us with offers of government meat or pizza made with cheese substitute. After all, being lunch ladies had to have some perks, right? And who could resist Chicken Giggles? It was "a giggling good time" according to the packaging. Seriously, who else could claim a more legitimate in with the government commodities man than us?

The *thwop, thwop* of the signs popping in the wind was both comforting in its steadiness and slightly annoying. Sam turned up the radio. The closer we got to Chicago, the more Chase Hatton music we started to hear. Our grins widened, and energy rose in us, surging like jolts of electricity. The thin straps of my tank left my arms bare. With the top down, the sun warmed my shoulders, but I worried about my 'do.

"Is the wind ruining my hair?"

She laughed, as my dark, curly hair was always a mess.

"Nah. You look great."

"Good. I have to look my best for Chase."

Sam and I both had the hots for Chase and tried to ignore the fact that he was married to the very beautiful and talented Hope Hatton. As traffic slowed to a near stop, I picked up on an earlier conversation.

"You know, it's just not fair. Why should a world-class photographer like Hope Hatton be allowed to wed a mega-rock-star like Chase? Shouldn't fame and fortune be spread out in order to keep the world in balance?"

"No kidding."

"You know, no more Nichole Kidmans and Tom Cruises—"

"Or Angelina Jolies and Brad Pitts."

"Exactly." I wracked my brain for any more celebrity couples. "No more Taylor Swift and... insert name of famous-person-of-the-week. It would be more equitable if Chase Hatton hooked up with, say, a lunch lady."

"True dat. We should start a movement."

"You know, we really should. Dani Hatton has a kind of ring to it. Don't you think?"

"Beautiful."

For the rest of the ride I let my fantasy play out in my head. Who wouldn't want a rock star for a husband? At least in fantasy land, where everyone was safe and rock stars were true to their partners.

* * *

After getting lost for a half-hour because we weren't listening to our GPS, we found our hotel. We checked in and went through the whole ritualistic reapplication of make-up and fluffing of hair. I brought the ingredients to make Nutty Irishmen and we both had glasses in front of us on the counter.

Sam went shopping with me the week before and helped me pick out a sheer black shirt to wear over a black cami. I had on the pair of jeans that made me somehow look tall and skinny. *Yep.* I turned sideways, admiring myself in the mirror. *I'm looking good.*

My gaze shifted to Sam's reflection. She was gorgeous. Blond, stacked, and vivacious—a dangerous combination. She could be wearing a nun's habit and still inspire men to drool and women to come unraveled; that was just Sam. I don't know how many times women threatened to kick our asses for speaking to their boyfriends. Or how many men I needed to talk off the ledge when they discovered she wouldn't be going home with them after last call. I was, in a word, my friend's keeper. It was a job I both loathed and loved.

I returned my attention to my reflection. In those few seconds I'd gone from hottie to hopeless. I sighed and picked up my drink, downing it.

"What's wrong?" She could always read me, but she'd blow it off if I told her. Tell me I'm crazy.

"Nothing. I'm getting myself another drink. Want one?"

"You finished your first already?" She added another quick mist of hairspray. "Nah. I'm good."

She was more of a beer-drinker anyway. But she'd always try whatever concoction I'd come up with. She was the best as a friend. Funny, willing to be silly at the drop of a hat, and loyal, always there for you. But there's only so much I could take of having a male approach our table and act like he's talking to the group while still, physically, turning his back on me to ogle my best bud. It was irritating. And even those with the strongest of egos—which I would never count myself among—would feel like a dumpy housewife who couldn't raise the hottie meter above a zero next to her.

Being thrown back into the dating scene with someone who was stunning was... nerve-wracking. How could I be expected to bring my game against the Serena Williams of the dating world?

It's not a competition.

Or is it?

Somehow, in my mind, this concert had become bigger than a concert. It was my debut, or my re-debut or something. I knew it was silly, but I couldn't help but obsess over it. Everything must go well. I'm not saying men needed to throw themselves at me and offer me marriage proposals, I simply needed to feel like, after all this time, I still had it.

And what if I didn't? I had a feeling if things didn't go well tonight, it would get harder and harder to put myself out there. Although I was a bundle of nerves, I felt something coming alive in me.

* * *

We caught a cab to the venue. Seconds before I handed our tickets to the person manning the turnstile, Samantha whispered in my ear, "Oh, and... Bill isn't really sure if these tickets are legit. But don't worry, we can buy some at the window if they're fake."

My whole life, or at least the last six years, I'd been dreaming about seeing Chase Hatton in concert. And now, right before my dream became a reality, she told me this? I handed the lady my ticket as Samantha whispered those fatal words, and I only had a heartbeat, an eternal heartbeat, to find out if my hopes were dashed. I rushed through the turnstile, all the while expecting to hear the lady calling me back, but all I heard was the blissful hum of the crowd around me.

I turned on Sam. "I can't believe you just told me that. We might not have gotten in at all."

She grabbed my arm and hustled me forward. "It was because I didn't want you to freak out like you are. Let's get you a beer."

We secured our brews and, as we turned away from

the counter, twenty dollars lighter in our pockets, Sam urged me forward. "Come on. We need to get armbands."

"Why?"

"Because, babe, our seats are on the floor."

"No shit?"

She grinned. "No shit."

Minutes later, armbands gracing our wrists, we headed along a hallway and up some stairs, juggling beer as people jostled us and jockeyed for position in the confined area. I'd been too nervous to eat all day, so my buzz came on fast. We stepped out into the auditorium, and the place pulsed with excitement. As my heart beat faster, I turned in a circle, drinking in the atmosphere. I realized after a second or two Sam was way ahead of me, so I jogged down the stairs after her. At the end of the seats was a half-wall. Security shined a flashlight on our armbands and we passed through an opening, wading out onto the floor.

Sam looked around. "Let's get a feel for the crowd here. Are these people going to be fun?" she said loudly. A few people turned and gave us cursory glances, then returned to their conversations. "Definitely not. Fun factor, zero. Come with me, drunk one."

She led me over to an area on the opposite side of the stage from where we entered. "What about you people? Are you fun?"

At this we got a few cheers and assertions of "we're the funnest damned people in the whole fucking auditorium."

"This is our spot," Sam said with a nod.

By the time Chase hit the stage our signs were beer-soaked and mangled underfoot. But he was as attractive and endearing as he seemed to be on TV, and he was funny, to boot. I tried to forget he wrote all of his songs for Hope, and imagined, instead, that he'd written them for me.

"Isn't he fantastic?" I yelled at Samantha.

She grabbed my hand. "Come on, girl." We stepped over our signs, and she dragged me through the crowd, which didn't exactly part like the Red Sea for us. I looked back at the people she elbowed out of the way and mouthed an apology as she pulled me farther in. When we stopped, I could touch the stage. I couldn't believe it. This close to Chase Hatton after all this time. Perhaps it was wrong for me to have a crush on a rock star at the age of twenty-eight, but it was a whole lot safer than falling in love with somebody real, so I took my rock star fantasy for what it was worth. With the combination of alcohol and adrenaline pumping through my system, and the heat brought on by too many bodies squashed together, my head was swimming, and I suddenly felt faint. I thought, through my mush-brain, "This isn't good. I'm going to pass out, and then people are going to trample me to death." The sickly sweet smell of hops and barley clouding the air didn't help either. Luckily, I held it together.

After the concert ended, Sam and I prepared to follow the crowd out. We overheard a couple of guys talking about partying with Chase Hatton. Naturally, we shadowed them, winding through corridors with scores of other people, until they sauntered through a gaggle of security guards and into a curtained off area. Chase was so close I could taste it.

"Sorry, lady. Can't let you back there."

"But you let those guys—"

"They have V.I.P. passes." Too late, as the last one went through The Holy Portal, I noticed the clear plastic pockets with credentials hanging around their necks.

I sighed. "Would it help to tell you as a lunch lady I have access to government meat?"

He shook his head with a smile.

"I figured as much." Some could be wooed by offers of government meat, some could not.

In desperation, I searched for another way in. Beyond the main entrance, a little farther down the hall, was another curtain, not guarded, underneath the concrete of some upper level seating. I headed in that direction. Checking over my shoulder, I grabbed Sam and ducked under the tarp. We were in the lower bowl. On the floor, roadies scurried around like ants on a discarded potato chip, hundreds of them, it seemed. Some carried cables, some equipment, some disassembled the rods holding the stage together. Sam and I watched for a while, fascinated, then remembered our mission.

I crept forward, peeling a vinyl tarp back a tad. In the middle of the five-by-five-foot area, a lone guard sat on a chair, but she seemed to be focused more on the main entrance to the room. I closed the curtain when she glanced in our direction, checking again after a few minutes. "She's still looking our way," I muttered to Sam.

She nodded solemnly. Though usually the one calling the shots in situations such as this, she could tell I was zeroed in on the prize, and didn't question me. I was bound and determined to get backstage and meet Chase. It wasn't like I wanted to kiss him, or maul him, or anything—although I certainly wouldn't object to having the opportunity to do that—it was just... I was compelled to meet him. I felt like we'd really get along well together. I was... slightly deranged.

I couldn't believe I was being so bold. I mean, I was Mrs. Rule Follower. I always stuck to the correct procedure when dropping my daughter Tabitha off at school or picking her up, to the consternation of all the other drivers. I never ripped off mattress tags and always counted my groceries to make sure I had less than twenty in the express lane. But in some situations, the rules didn't apply, and this was one of them.

Seconds later, our golden opportunity came. "Come on. She's facing the other way." I ran on tiptoes right past the guard, into a little front room, with Samantha on my heels, tripping across the floor like Fred Flintstone and Barney Rubble.

We giggled quietly and scoped out the area. The room was empty, barren of everything save some computer printed signs for the opening groups, and one for Chase. "They must have had a meet-and-greet in here earlier," I surmised. It was stuffy and closed feeling. Seeing another exit out of the room, I tugged Samantha along. More signs and arrows with the bands' names graced the walls, and a gridded metal staircase descended into the bowels of the auditorium, turning 180 degrees at the landing. I followed this down, my heart rate soaring. It got cooler with each step and the air felt more alive. We were backstage. This was awesome! Awesome until...

...we were spotted by a roadie with a length of cable slung over his shoulder. He stood in a wide tunnel, of sorts, already filling up with equipment which had been lugged off stage. The roadie was good-looking and seemed rather clean-cut for a member of a rock-and-roll stage crew. His hair, however, was long enough to fall into his face, partially blocking his—I couldn't help but notice—fetchingly green-grey eyes. He was tan, and with his blond hair, more closely resembled a surfer-boy than a roadie. In fact, that image was so strong I could almost see a surfboard balanced where the cable was. Jeans and a black T-shirt graced his ripped body. Muscular arms shone with sweat as he peered up at us, frozen near the bottom of the steps. "Ladies..." he scolded, shaking his head. He laid the cable on a cart, which already had a pair of huge speakers on it, and crossed his hands over his chest as he turned back around. "You two are not supposed to be here."

"Uh, yeah," I answered lamely. "We... uh... got lost. We were supposed to be at a party backstage, and we were trying to find a bathroom. Then we got turned around. Right, Samantha?"

"Yeah. We're bad with directions."

Remembering our circuitous route to the hotel earlier, I sputtered. I tried to hold it in, but I couldn't and burst into a full out laugh.

"All right, ladies." He gave us a good-natured grin, spreading his arms out to herd us back up the stairs. "I think you'd better go now." He had a nice voice, soothing.

"Oh, sure. Oh, you want us to go this way." I continued to fake being lost, even though Mr. Handsome obviously pegged us.

I glanced back when we reached the landing. He had his hands resting on the stair's railings and was hanging his head between them, laughing at us. Looking up, he caught my eye, and I was breathless. He was so unbelievably hot. Sam clamored on up ahead of me, unaware I had stopped. The nameless roadie and I stared at each other for several seconds before I forced myself to speak.

"Goodbye," I murmured, wondering over the tug of regret gripping my core. He straightened, and I worried he could hear the blood pounding through my veins. I got the feeling he might be different from what you would expect from someone in the rock world. Maybe not simply out for a good time like they all seemed to be. There was more to him somehow. As strange as it sounds, through even our brief encounter, I got the feeling when he played, he played for keeps.

"See ya." He flashed an easy grin, his teeth extraordinarily white. I turned and hurried after Sam. We scooted past security again then headed back into the main corridor.

Sam exhaled. "Okay, what now?"

I wondered what the roadie's story was. "Hmm?"

"In your grand scheme to meet Chase? Where to now?"

"Oh, umm..."

"You're not giving up because that guy caught us are you?"

Was I?

"No. No, of course not. There has to be a way. Let's walk on and see if we can find another entrance."

"Okay, but these shoes have to go." She slipped off her cheetah-skin heels.

"Good thinking, girlfriend." I smiled, putting our run-in with the roadie behind us. I yanked off my boots, and we both rolled up our jeans, giving our sleazy rock and roll outfits an air of Elly May Clampett. We strolled—Samantha barefoot, me in black thigh-highs—around the auditorium.

When we passed a group of guys, we heard them say Chase and the band were going to Shoeless Joe's across the street. Score! We did an about face and headed for an exit.

* * *

Shoeless Joe's was packed. We waded upstream to get a drink at the bar then got a spot, of sorts, where we could lean against a brass railing near the dance floor. A group of guys standing next to us cast glances our way. Sam started complaining about how much her feet hurt. Mine ached, too. My ankles were weak and wobbled like I'd been ice skating all night. My toes rivaled for the title of King of Pain. Not only were they crammed into narrow confines, but the majority of my weight was concentrated on them, and the balls of my feet burned where they made contact with the boots.

One of the men, who wore a tan sports coat and a receding hairline, cooed at Samantha, ushering her over to a stool he'd found somewhere. "Come here, beautiful. I'll massage your feet for you." And without further ado, he did just that. His circle opened to allow me in. Sam was in her element now, surrounded by interested men, which was repetitive since any man would be interested around her.

A cute, shorter guy in a long, black coat shook our hands. "Hi. I'm Kyle."

Sam let out a yelp, examining her feet. "Ouch! You bit me. I can't believe you bit me!" She yanked her toe out of the man's mouth—the man who from then on out became forever known as Terry the Toe-Sucker—and started to rub it. "Geez! That hurt."

Terry the Toe-Sucker drew her off to one side, presumably to apologize. I kept my eye on her.

"So, are you girls from here?" Kyle was asking.

"Uhh, what? Oh. No. We're from Bloomington. About two hours from here." I craned my neck to see around someone who obstructed my view of Sam. "We're lunch ladies," I threw out in way of explanation.

The girls always laughed that I inserted this into any early conversation with people we met at the bars. It was a good opener. People always had strong feelings about lunch ladies, either good or bad, and it was sort of a funny job.

"Really?" Kyle seemed interested, although his eyes kept going to Samantha. "Can I get you another drink?"

"Sure. Thanks."

"What are you drinking?"

"I'm switching to tequila."

His eyebrows rose, and he gave me a nod as a sign of respect. "And Samantha?"

I was impressed he remembered her name.

"She'll take a Miller Lite."

He smiled at that and started fighting his way to the bar.

Another one of the guys stepped into the conversational void Kyle left, introducing himself. I don't remember exactly what his name was, but he was cute, with curly hair. He became, for reasons that will be shared later, Mr. Handsy, or, at times, The Guy with the Hands. As it turned out, our whole group was made up of Canadian hockey referees, although I didn't detect an accent among them.

The bar was playing Chase Hatton music, and not only the songs played on the radio, either, but even obscure ones. Of course, I knew all the words, and, perhaps because of the shot of tequila I downed, I kept saying—rather loudly, I think—"This is a great song!" The Guy with the Hands started singing one of the songs with me, and, impressed by his knowledge and plain excited someone else knew one, I started singing and dancing with him.

Then he did the strangest thing. He put his hands under my hair and lifted it as he massaged my neck and scalp. It felt incredible, like all the nerve endings up there had rolled over and gone to sleep. His hands were strong, masterful, as he worked my tired muscles. So, this strange man was running his hands through my hair and I was letting him. I couldn't help myself. It felt so good, and I simply melted into it.

He put his hands on my hips, and my heart rate ticked upward. An instant sweat coated my palms, and my stomach began a quiet but persistent rebellion. On the pretense of telling Sam something, I moved away. But he must have shifted too, because later he was behind me, dancing and drawing me into him by the hips, singing again, in my ear. A little flattered someone seemed to be into me and not Samantha, I didn't move away at first. Then, as a joke, Kyle and The Quiet One—one of the refs who hadn't said more than a few words all night—came over and sandwiched me, pretending—poorly—that they knew the words, too.

All of a sudden, from out of nowhere, some strange guy from another table broke in, grabbed me, and started dancing. "That's my wife," he yelled. His friends laughed. He let go of me and stumbled back to his table, but his words were like a slap in the face.

"Sam, let's go to the bathroom." She was being monopolized by Terry, who didn't seem at all her type. She usually went for the young, buff guys. A body was very important to her. I found out later she spent most of the evening stroking the poor guy's ego.

"I'm good-looking, right? You're into me?" Little did he know he stood a snowball's chance in Tahiti with my gorgeous girlfriend.

I practically ran into the bathroom, Sam on my heels. I rushed to the sink, gripping the sides, the cool porcelain bracing.

"What's wrong?"

"I don't know."

"Bullshit. What's wrong? Did you have too much to drink? Are you feeling sick?"

I couldn't tell her the truth, that the guy pretending to be my husband brought on a wave of guilt so strong it swamped me. "Yeah. Well, sort of. Just really hot."

She ripped a paper towel from the holder and wet it, holding it to my forehead. I closed my eyes and breathed deeply, not allowing myself to think. *Breathe in, breathe out. You are not going to fall apart. You came here to have fun, and damn it, you're going to have fun. Even if it kills you. It's been five years since Darren died. You need to get over it.* I breathed in and breathed out. I thought of my daughter, Tabitha. I missed her. She was probably home in bed in her cupcake pajamas. You couldn't get the things off her. I smiled and opened my eyes.

"I'm better," I said weakly.

Sam still frowned. "Are you sure?"

The blood returned to my face. "Yeah. I don't want to ruin everything for you."

"What? Are you kidding?" Sam inspected herself in the mirror and messed with her hair for a second before turning to me. "These guys are shady."

"Do you think so? They seem pretty harmless."

"Oh, no. They are shady all the way. I can't believe he stuck my sweaty, dirty toe into his mouth. I mean, we were walking all over the auditorium. Who knows what I picked up on my feet?"

I chuckled. "Did he really hurt you?"

"Yeah! Bastard. Hurt like hell." She slipped her foot out of the pumps, swinging her size nine up on the sink. "I can't see any marks though."

"Are you sure he doesn't have rabies?"

She laughed. "I wouldn't put it past him. That Kyle is kind of cute, though."

I glanced in the mirror. All of the evening's activities had taken the life out of my hair. I caught her eye in the reflection. "I think he likes you, too."

She ignored that remark and slipped her shoe back on. "Are you sure you're okay now?"

"Nothing another shot won't cure." I hooked my arm through hers and tried to give her a reassuring smile. "You know," I raised my eyebrows, "Chase could be arriving at any minute. Let's get out there, Toots."

ABOUT THE AUTHOR

M.J. Schiller is a lunch lady/romance-romantic suspense writer. She enjoys writing novels whose characters include rock stars, desert princes, teachers, futuristic Knights, construction workers, cops, and a wide variety of others. In her mind everybody has a romance. She is the mother of a twenty-two-year-old and three twenty-year-olds. That's right, triplets! So having recently taught four children to drive, she likes to escape from life on occasion by pretending to be a rock star at karaoke. However…you won't be seeing her name on any record labels soon.

ROMANTIC REALMS COLLECTION:

TAKEN BY STORM
AN UNCOMMON LOVE
LEAP INTO THE KNIGHT
LADY OF THE KNIGHT
A KNIGHT TO REMEMBER

ROCKING ROMANCE COLLECTION:

TRAPPED UNDER ICE,
ABANDON ALL HOPE,
BETWEEN ROCK AND A HARD PLACE,
ROCK ME, GENTLY

REAL ROMANCE COLLECTION:

UPON A MIDNIGHT CLEAR

THE HEART TEACHES BEST
DAMAGE DONE
HOMETOWN HEARTACHE
TAKE A CHANCE ON ME

DEVILISH DIVAS COLLECTION:

TO HELL IN A COACH BAG
DAMNED IF I DO
THE DEVIL YOU KNOW

www.ingramcontent.com/pod-product-compliance
Lightning Source LLC
Chambersburg PA
CBHW051437170626
46809CB00006B/2499